CW01667903

My mission is to create sickle cell awareness, I have jumped out of a plane, swam with sharks and even run a ten and five-thousand-mile race for the sickle cell Society, London. Writing this fictional love story is my way of explaining the effects of sickle cell anaemia in the simplest way possible while enjoying a love story. The storyline is set in Nigeria, London and Italy. Fasten your seatbelts and enjoy the ride.

Printed in Great Britain

To Shaleen
Lots of love
Peace
x

In Loving Memory of my friend Bunmi Fadipe, who died on the 15th of March 2016 due to complications of sickle cell anaemia.

Chapter One

It's the start of the summer holidays and Lola is wondering what she will do with the rest of her life. Lola didn't get the grades she needed to go to the University of her choice and she didn't want to re-take the exams. Lola's father wasn't all that bothered about her not getting the grades to go to University; he wanted her to get married; he had been plotting the union between Lola and his best friend's son Tunde. Lola and Tunde have known each other all their lives, and they got on well. Tunde was an intelligent student, he passed all his exams, and he gained admission into the University of Ibadan to study Mechanical Engineering. Lola and Tunde are out walking and talking about their future. Lola is overjoyed that Tunde is now going to the University of Ibadan. The thought of Tunde being in a different State played on her mind. It was Tunde's intention to go to the University of Lagos; he ended up applying for the University of Ibadan when he realised that Lola had changed her mind about going to University. Tunde didn't want to be too far away from his future wife. Lola is such a tall and stunning girl; she turned the heads of all the boys in high school. She dated the State Governor's Son Wale; her dad did not approve of him. Wale is a lady's man, he is handsome and his father is very wealthy. Wale liked Lola a lot, and she liked him too, she had kept her relationship with Wale low key because she knew her father didn't like him.

Most of the girls in the local area were envious of Lola. Wale could be out on a date with another girl, as soon as he clapped eyes on Lola, he would ignore his date and talk to her. Lola still had feelings for Wale, and she loved the attention he gave her. Wale's mother lived in America, every time he returned from visiting his mother, he would buy expensive gifts for her. Lola ended up breaking off the relationship with Wale, she could no longer put up with his womanising. Wale was not too pleased that she dumped him.

One sunny afternoon while Lola was at the market with her mother, Dupe approached Lola. Dupe is a very attractive young girl and well known for her arrogance, she told Lola to stay away from Wale. 'Wale is my boyfriend, you better stop trying to seduce him, Wale loves me,' shouted Dupe. Lola told Dupe to take it up with Wale, as she tried to walk away, Dupe slapped Lola across the face, she grabbed hold of Dupe's arm then they fought. Her mother was so cross; she broke up the fight with the help of the other women. Dupe got told off for disrespecting Lola's mother. 'Dupe, how could you fight Lola in front of her mother?' Asked one woman. She ignored the question, she had scratch marks on her face and a bloody lip, Dupe was crying not because of her wounds, but because she had come off worse from the fight, she didn't think Lola had it in her to fight her. Lola looked so gentle; her peers called her Aje Bota. (A spoilt child) Dupe warned Lola again, to stay away from Wale or she would not hear the last of this. Lola's mother was so disappointed in Lola and told her to stay away from Wale and Dupe. Dupe's grandfather is an herbalist; she didn't want him to cast a spell on Lola.

Wale found out about the fight between Dupe and Lola from one of his housemaids. The housemaid was at the market and she saw them fighting. Wale turned up at Lola's house to apologise to Lola and her mother. Lola's father asked Wale to leave his house and warned him never to come anywhere near his daughter again.

Lola also wanted nothing to do with Wale; his womanising was becoming tiresome. This incident with Dupe was one of many problems she had with Wale's many girlfriends. Wale was angry with Dupe, he went straight round to her house and told her never to speak to him again. Dupe was crying her eyes out, she blamed Lola for their break-up, Dupe's mother was angry about the incident and its believed Dupe's mother asked her father to put a curse on Lola. Two days later, Dupe bumped into Lola in the street and she cursed at Lola and told her she would never find happiness.

Chapter Two

Lola attended a fashion school in the city, she is an outstanding dressmaker. She had always designed her own clothes. Lola's mother bought Lola a sewing machine, and she sewed for the people in the local area, her designs are trendy and people patronised her, she made enough money to buy two more sewing machines. She took on two apprentices and taught them the trade. Lola's reputation for being a brilliant dressmaker preceded her. A year later she won the contract to sew Wale's older brother's wife's wedding attire. Wale had moved to America; he gained admission to Harvard to study Law. Dupe ended up marrying a local businessman, they had two girls, her husband wanted a male child, so he took on a mistress who gave birth to twin boys. The mistress argued with Dupe, she even told her to take her girls and leave. Dupe's husband kept taking sides with his mistress so, she decided she would no longer stay under the same roof with her husband's mistress; she took her children and moved back to her parent's house. Dupe's husband gave her money to open a restaurant; he did that to help ease his conscience for the way he treated her; he didn't want his girls to want for nothing. Dupe ran a successful business; the rumour is that her grandfather did a spell that made people patronise her restaurant. People came from far and wide to eat at her restaurant.

Wale's brother's wedding appeared in all the fashion magazines in Lagos; Lola received many orders from the rich and famous in Lagos. The governor of Ibadan gave Alhaji Lola's contact detail. Alhaji asked Lola to come to Lagos; he wanted her to do the designs for his Son's wedding. Alhaji's son is getting married to the Lagos governor's daughter.

Lola arrived in Lagos to meet Alhaji in his office in Lekki. The building is massive; inside the building the marble flooring was shining in the sunlight. Lola compared Alhaji's office to the Oval Office in the White House, she had seen the film Independence Day. Lola noticed all the affluent people Alhaji had taken photographs with, there is a picture of him and ex-President, Goodluck Jonathan. Alhaji's office decor is breath-taking, you can tell no expense was spared on the decor. Lola was uncomfortable sitting in Alhaji's office. Alhaji looked like he was in his early sixties. You could tell he was a handsome man when he was younger, he looked at Lola over his spectacles that made her feel more uncomfortable. Alhaji told Lola to relax that, he would make her a wealthy woman. Lola smiled in appreciation. Alhaji gave Lola the address to his house; he asked her to go see his wife, she would be the one to give her instructions about the designs of the outfits she was to make. Alhaji owned a shopping complex in Victoria Island. Alhaji's wife took her to see the complex and showed Lola, her new fashion designing premises. Lola couldn't believe her eyes, everything was moving too fast, she was fearful that she would open her eyes, and everything would be back to normal.

Chapter Three

Tunde graduated from the University of Ibadan with honours; he decided not to continue with his master's due to his father's sudden death. His mother never spoke of his father's death, and Tunde couldn't get his head around his father's sudden death, he was healthy although; he complained about constant pains. Tunde remembers his father when he was sometimes bedridden for days in pain. Tunde's father was health-conscious; he was always particular about his diet; he drank lots of water, he always kept himself hydrated and he tried not to overexert himself. Every year without fail, he would go to the hospital for a health check.

Tunde's father attended a meeting in Lagos Island. After the meeting, Tunde's father went to see Lola and Tunde at the shopping complex. He told them he secured a new contract with a major company in China. Tunde's father was proud of his achievement because he worked so hard to secure this deal. Tunde's father was eager to get back to Ibadan; he had another meeting scheduled there. On the Ibadan expressway, he had a blowout. Tunde's father got out of the car and stood in the heavy rain while the driver changed the tyre. The driver finished changing the tyre; then they started on their way again. When Tunde's father got home, he changed out of his wet clothes and took a quick shower as he was getting ready; he felt pains in his legs, he could not move, he sat on the bed and reached for his medication; he lay down for a while hoping that the pain would subside. The pain did not subside; he shouted out to his wife, by this time the pain was now in his chest, he was finding it difficult to breathe, he later passed out. His wife ran for help, Tunde's father was now in a coma, he never came around from the coma. The cause of death was hyperthermia.

Tunde's father ran a reputable company dealing with mobile phones. He had built the company from scratch; and he trusted no one to get involved with his business, because in the past, he had trusted a good friend of his, but his friend was stealing money from him and going behind his back to undercut him with his business clients. He got rid of his business partner and he worked alone. The company was failing because no one knew anything about his business transactions. Tunde's mother had no choice but to sell the business. Things were difficult for them, Tunde relied on his father to pay his University fee, he was in his final year at University and he was struggling to keep up with all the University fee and payments. Lola took on most of the financial burden. Tunde joined Lola in Lagos; she was doing well. Lola was living in one of Alhaji's prestigious properties in Victoria Gardens. Lola couldn't believe how much her luck had changed. Alhaji used his influence to get a Mechanical Engineering job for Tunde, no one knows why Alhaji took a shine to Lola, there was a rumour he always wanted a daughter, his son was his only child. Alhaji and his wife had the sickle cell trait. The good Lord gave them a child who did not have sickle cell anaemia, he vowed that he would not tempt fate by having another child. Alhaji's wife told Lola that she looked so much like Alhaji's mother, she showed her a picture; Lola was the spitting image of Alhaji's mother.

The following year Tunde and Lola got married, Alhaji spared no expense on the wedding. Alhaji invited all the elite and influential people in the country to the wedding, it was a grand occasion. Both Lola's parents and Tunde's mother attended. Alhaji gave the deeds to the house in

Victoria Gardens to Tunde and Lola as a wedding present. Tunde and Lola were both successful in their businesses. Tunde was envious of the attention Alhaji gave Lola; he tried to drive a wedge between them. Tunde complained about how much time Lola was spending with Alhaji and his wife, his mother kept implying that something was going on and that Tunde should keep a close eye on them both. Deep down Tunde knew his wife was not having an affair with Alhaji but, his mother kept messing with his head. Tunde's paranoia was causing a rift between them. Lola had no choice but, to reduce the time she spent with Alhaji and his wife. It was such a shame because they both treated Lola like the daughter they never had.

Six months later Lola fell pregnant; Tunde was over the moon when he realised she was having a boy. Lola had to cut down on the time she spent at work, she was ill and felt tired all the time. Lola was finding the pregnancy very difficult, she couldn't wait to give birth. Tunde stopped Lola from going to work; her doctor asked her to take it easy due to her high blood pressure, she can work from home there was no need for her to go to work, Lola is lucky to have the best dressmakers working for her.

Lola gave birth to a bouncing baby boy, he looked just like his father. Tunde's mother came to Lagos to help with the baby, Lola wanted her own mother to come and stay and look after her and the baby. Tunde's mother spent most of her time in Lagos after the death of her husband, she was always interfering with Lola and Tunde's relationship. Lola was sick of her interference; she wanted nothing to do with her. Tunde named his son Babatunde Jr after his grandfather. Babatunde means "father returns". Babatunde was about three months old when Lola noticed that her baby's fingers and feet had swollen, and he would not stop crying. Lola took her baby to Britannia Hospital to have him checked over after many blood tests; the doctor told Lola the devastating news that Babatunde has sickle cell anaemia. Lola was so confused; she didn't know what sickle cell anaemia was, the doctor was trying to explain but, she couldn't comprehend. The doctor requested that she called her husband, Tunde's mother sat in the doctor's office; she knows what sickle cell anaemia is. Tunde's mother was crying and shouting in Yoruba 'I am in trouble today'. Lola was looking at her mother-in-law, wondering why she kept saying that. Lola was too distressed; she chose not to take any notice of her mother-in-law and her antics. Tunde arrived at the doctor's office. The doctor wanted to know if sickle cell anaemia was in the family. No, they both said. Tunde looked at his mother for reassurance, she sat there talking to herself. The doctor told them that sickle cell anaemia is hereditary, so they both have the trait. The doctor gave them all the advice on how to look after their baby. When Tunde got home, he was so angry; he wanted to know why Lola didn't tell him she had a blood disease. Lola cried, 'why didn't you tell me you had sickle cell anaemia?' Asked Lola. 'I don't have sickle cell anaemia, you were so desperate to get married, how am I sure he is my child?' Asked Tunde. All along his mother sat crying in the corner, Lola was so angry; she couldn't believe Tunde had accused her of infidelity. By this time, he was spitting venom, he even had the audacity to accuse her of having an affair with Alhaji. Lola stormed out of the room to attend to her crying baby and call her mother. While Lola was out of the room, Tunde's mother told Tunde that his father died from complications of sickle cell anaemia. Tunde was not sure whether he was angry about the fact that his mother kept this vital information from him or the fact she had sat there while he accused Lola of all sorts.

Lola was on the phone to her mother sobbing, her mother was in shock, Lola's mother couldn't remember anyone in the family having sickle cell anaemia. She told her daughter to take it easy with Tunde that he is in shock and he will soon realise he is being unreasonable. Lola said she didn't think she could forgive Tunde for all the ugly things he had said to her, her father came into the room and wanted to know what the matter was. Lola's mother told her husband the devastating news about Babatunde having sickle cell anaemia, it came as a shock, he couldn't think of anyone in his family who has or had sickle cell, her father was furious; he told his wife they are both going to Lagos to get tested, he wanted to sort this out once and for all.

Lola's Mother and father were at the Lagos teaching hospital for a genotype test, he was not prepared to let his daughter get blamed for something that was not her fault. Sickle cell anaemia is a hereditary blood disorder; it's passed down from your parents. Lola was a very healthy child, so she couldn't have sickle cell anaemia. The doctor asked Lola's parents to come into his office. He told them that Lola's father's blood type is AS, so he has the sickle cell trait, but, his wife as the normal AA blood type. He explained the process to them. The doctor told them that to inherit sickle cell anaemia, you would need to receive a pair of mutated genes – one mutated gene from your mother and from your father. If you only receive one mutated gene, you won't have sickle cell anaemia; just a carrier known as the sickle cell trait. If both you and your partner have the sickle cell trait, there's a fifty-fifty percent chance that one or all your children will inherit a pair of mutated genes and develop sickle cell anaemia. People with the sickle cell trait do not have serious health issues, but they should avoid getting dehydrated and not overexert themselves. The doctor also said this is the reason he always insists on screening before marriage. Tunde and Lola had their genotypes tested; they booked the test due, to their constant arguing. The doctor confirmed that they both have the trait. Lola parents wanted to know why Tunde's mother did not take the test. She kept making excuses for not doing so, Tunde also kept making excuses for his mother not taking the test. Lola's father accused Tunde's mother of knowing they had the blood disorder in the family and that, was the reason Tunde's father insisted their children marry each other. Tunde's mother cried, 'How dare you speak ill of the dead,' she said. Lola's mother asked, 'what killed your husband?' Tunde's mother was still crying as she walked out of the room. Lola's mother told Tunde that she believes his father died of sickle cell anaemia, she remembered back then when he came to visit he was often in pain, we thought nothing of it. Lola's mother looked at her husband for reassurance, remember the time you were at that meeting at Ilesha, he complained of severe pain. You had to take him home, he could just about walk, he was in pain for several days, according to his wife. No wonder Tunde is their only child. 'Tunde is not their only child; he has a sister,' replied Lola. Forget this wicked family, we need to get back to Ibadan, we need to get Lola's brother, and sister tested. We cannot go through this again. Lola escorted her parents to their car where the driver was waiting, she pleaded with her parents not to forget to get her siblings tested.

Lola wanted her mother-in-law to leave; she never liked her anyway and she no longer trusted her around her or her child. Tunde's mother knew how to handle Babatunde when he was in pain, she had special herbs that, she would use, and the herbs seemed to work. Tunde's mother's knowledge about Babatunde illness made Lola more suspicious that, she had cared for someone with sickle cell anaemia but, Tunde refused to talk about it.

Lola was running late for a very important meeting with Alhaji; he wanted to introduce her to one of his contacts from London. The contact owned a top fashion outlet in London and was looking for a new supplier. Lola kissed her son goodbye; Babatunde, is now three years old and attends a private nursery called Cypress Bay International School in Lekki. Lola had met with the owner of the school to discuss her child's needs. The owner is a qualified child specialist and understood the effects of sickle cell anaemia; she recognised the signs if Babatunde was not feeling well. Lola felt comfortable leaving her child in the care of the school. Tunde's mother collected Babatunde from school with the driver. It had been raining all day, Tunde's mother and Babatunde made a dashed for the front door; she didn't want her grandson to get wet. After Babatunde had his dinner, he complained about pains in his legs. Tunde's mother massaged his legs for him and gave him two pain relief tablets to help suppress his pain. The pain was getting worse; he was now crying, she reached for her mobile phone to call Lola to tell her she was taking Babatunde to the hospital. The phone just kept ringing then it went to voicemail. Tunde's mother left a message, telling her to meet them at the hospital, she rang her son and had to leave him a message too. By the time they got to the hospital due to the rush hour traffic, Babatunde had passed out, the pain was unbearable, she was calling both Lola and Tunde. The doctor saw Babatunde, they did their best to revive him, he had a stroke and stopped breathing. Tunde's mother was inconsolable; she couldn't believe she had lost another loved one to sickle cell anaemia. The doctors had to sedate her.

Tunde was in meetings all afternoon, he checked his phone at the end of his final meeting, he saw all his mother's missed calls. He returned his mother's phone call, and a nurse answered the phone and asked him to come to the hospital, she wouldn't give him any more information. Tunde was sick with worry; it felt like a long drive to the hospital. Tunde called Lola; she had just walked through the door, Lola had forgotten her phone at home; she was in such a hurry in the morning. Lola was on her way to the hospital too, 'have you spoken to your mother?' Asked Lola. 'No, a nurse answered the phone and refused to tell me anything,' he replied. Tunde met Lola outside the hospital; she could not drive to the hospital, she had to take a taxi because she was so worried and didn't know what to think. Babatunde had been in and out of the hospital, but this time it felt different. Lola ran into Tunde's arms, crying her eyes out, even though she was three months pregnant, they have been distant with each other. After finding out that Babatunde had sickle cell anaemia, it had caused so many arguments and led them to mistrust each other. Tunde kept himself so busy at work; he couldn't get over the guilt about his father having sickle cell anaemia and keeping his mother's secret. It left a permanent strain on the marriage. When Lola found out she was pregnant again, they talked about the chances their baby might have sickle cell anaemia. Tunde said it didn't matter and he would love this child as much as he loves Babatunde. Lola believed he said it out of guilt but, she felt the same. Looking after a child with sickle cell anaemia can be emotionally exhausting for the parents, Lola was in and out of the hospital with Babatunde. A nurse met them at the entrance; Lola noticed the tears in her eyes. Lola knew what had happened. The nurse rushed them into the doctor's office. The doctor gave them the sad news of their son's passing. Lola wasn't interested in Dr Ken's explanation; she couldn't believe her son was no more. Lola was crying, Tunde was trying to console her. Lola felt so alone and empty, she could hear Dr Ken telling her to think of the unborn baby she was carrying. All she could think of was Babatunde's handsome face. Lola had this sudden urge to be with her son. 'I need to see Babatunde, he is all alone and needs his mother.' Dr Ken said it was not a good idea for her to go to the mortuary. Lola stormed out of the doctor's office; she didn't know where the mortuary was. Lola was just opening every door as she walked down the corridor calling out her son's name. One door she opened, she saw a familiar face, it was her mother-in-law. Tunde's mother was now sitting on the bed still crying. Lola walked up to her and screamed at her 'why did you let my son die?' Asked Lola. Tunde's mother looked up and just kept on apologising. Lola turned away and continued her search for her son. Dr Ken caught up with Lola at the end of the corridor; he tried talking to her but, she became hysterical. Dr Ken had no choice but to sedate her. When she woke up Tunde and his mother was sitting beside her bed. Tunde looked so old; it seemed as if in the last four hours he had aged. She wondered why she married him, if not for their father's, she would have married

Wale. Lola was thinking what her life would have been like if she had gone to America with Wale, she had feelings for Wale but, she loved Tunde more. Wale had called her several times from America, he couldn't stop thinking about her. Wale, called Lola and asked her to divorce Tunde and come to America and marry him, she declined his offer and told him she loves Tunde. Lola didn't hear from Wale for a long time, he had called to tell her he was getting married to an American girl, and that was the last time she heard from him. Lola cried herself to sleep when she woke up again, Tunde's mother had gone home. Lola turned to her husband and asked, 'If his father died of sickle cell anaemia?' Tunde no longer wanted to keep his mother's secret, he wanted to tell Lola the truth the day he found out, but he promised his mother. Lola already knew the answer; she wanted to hear him say it. Tunde took her hand and said, he was sorry for all the heartache he had put her through, Lola just looked at him; then she asked him to leave she needed to be on her own.

Babatunde's burial was private; it was just close friends and family, Alhaji and his wife attended. They had been a great comfort to Lola after the death of her son. If she wasn't at work, she was at Alhaji's house. Tunde didn't complain about the time she spent there; he knew he wasn't able to give her the comfort she needed, and he didn't want to upset her anymore. Tunde's mother went back to Ibadan; there was no need for her to stay in Lagos since the house was always empty. Tunde stayed at work and Lola stayed away too, Lola never confronted her; she didn't want to give her mother-in-law the opportunity to make up any excuses.

Six months later Lola gave birth to another baby boy; Lola didn't get attached to the baby; for fear, he might die. Lola's mother came to stay and look after the new-born baby. Lola was suffering from postnatal depression, she could not get close to her baby, she was in constant fear that her baby would die. After sixteen weeks, the blood test result confirmed that her son is just a carrier of the blood disorder, he did not have sickle cell anaemia.

Chapter Four

After the death of Babatunde, the doctor diagnosed Tunde's mother with hypertension. Tunde spent a lot of time visiting his mother in Ibadan due to her ill health.

Lola was getting better; she was now showing affection towards her baby. Lola vowed never to forget Babatunde and that, Temi could never take his place, but she loved Temi all the same. Tunde was spending a lot of time in Ibadan; he used his mother's illness to stay away. Lola didn't care whether he was at home; she was finding it difficult to forgive him. Lola's mother spoke to her daughter about it; she told her she would have to forgive him or divorce him. They couldn't keep living the way they did; their relationship was distant, and they now slept in different rooms. Lola promised to sort it out with Tunde when he returns from Ibadan. Deep down, she still loved Tunde. Tunde was in Ibadan attending to his mother; she was admitted in hospital with high blood pressure. Tunde was her only child, so he was the only one she could rely on, his mother refused to come to Lagos; she still felt guilty for the death of Babatunde. His mother needed provisions, so he went to the supermarket to buy them. As he was leaving, he bumped into Dupe; she owned the restaurant next door. She embraced him and asked about Lola and the family. Dupe invited him for a drink; he told her he needed to get back to the hospital to attend to his mother. Dupe asked how his mother was doing and she promised to visit his mother at the hospital.

Dupe was a regular visitor at Tunde's mother's house. Tunde's mother liked Dupe a lot, she thought of Dupe as the daughter she never had. Dupe went on a date with Tunde; the date was engineered by his mother. Tunde asked after her husband; she told him he died in a car accident three years ago, her husband and his sons were on their way to a birthday party when a lorry crashed into them, she and her two daughters inherited all her husband's wealth. Tunde spent more time with Dupe, Dupe found so much pleasure in knowing she could take Lola's husband away from her. She still believes that Lola caused her breakup with Wale and she could never forgive her for that. Lola noticed that her husband was spending too much time in Ibadan, she knew his mother was not well, but his concern for her was out of the ordinary. Lola was not concerned about why Tunde spent too much time in Ibadan; she was more concerned about why he was neglecting his business in Lagos. The manager dealt with all the important meetings and decisions making for the business. The manager was always coming to the house to drop off the minutes of the meetings held, paperwork and cheques for Tunde to sign. Tunde was not paying attention to paperwork and signing of cheques without knowing what they were for.

Lola took her mother's advice and agreed to talk to her husband when he returned from Ibadan; she was now so desperate for them to get their marriage back on track. She loved her husband, but she was still grieving and seemed to have pushed her husband away. Later that evening, Lola's mother called and told her that her father is ill, and he is in hospital. Her father had not been right since the death of his grandson. Lola's father blamed himself for forcing Tunde and Lola together. Tunde's father was his best friend; he should have known something was wrong with him. Looking back, he remembered that his friend showed all the signs of having sickle cell anaemia. Tunde's father watched what he ate, he was always sick during the rainy season, he never played football with them when they were younger; he was always thirsty and drank water like a fish. Lola's father had gone to see his friend at home, his wife would make excuses, so no one could see her husband when he was sick. Lola's father remembered the day he went to visit Tunde's father at home, Tunde's mother was out, he was in no fit state to send his friend away. He was lying down on the bed, the pain in his legs was unbearable. Lola's father noticed all the Penicillin and Folic Acid beside his bed. Again, Lola's father thought nothing of it.

Lola understood the urgency in her mother's voice. Even though her mother didn't say it, she knew if she didn't leave for Ibadan today, she would never see her father alive again. She called the driver and told him to get ready to take her to Ibadan. The driver was not happy because; it was so late in the evening for them to be going to Ibadan; he went to get the car ready. Lola tried to call her husband; the phone just kept ringing, she couldn't leave a message. That was another thing she had noticed, Tunde had removed the voice message service from his phone. She kept calling him for the two hours' drive to Ibadan. Lola went straight to the hospital as soon as she got to her father's bedside, he opened his eyes and saw her standing there, he smiled and said in Yoruba ‘my daughter, please forgive me.’ That was Lola’s father’s final words, she hugged her father and told him she will always love him and that she had nothing to forgive him for. Lola sat and cried at her father’s bedside until the undertakers came to take him to the mortuary. Her mother was crying too; she had lost her soul mate. Lola went back to her mother’s house, they both held each other and cried. Lola’s brother was on the phone, trying to get hold of the rest of the family members. Just after Midnight, Lola remembered that she could not get hold of her husband, it wasn’t normal for him not to call her, she didn’t believe her husband had not seen all her missed calls. The news of her father’s passing was not something she could do over the phone, she tried to sleep, but she couldn’t sleep. Lola’s mother told her to lie down with her baby. Lola was so tired, but she didn’t want to leave her mother on her own, her mother insisted, she said she would appreciate the time alone. Lola must have drifted off for a moment; she woke up with sweat pouring off her body. The power supply had gone off. The power supply in Ibadan was not stable; to be honest, it is not stable in any part of Nigeria. Lola tried to keep her baby cool by fanning him to sleep, then she drifted off to sleep again.

Lola went to her mother-in-law's house; her mother-in-law seemed agitated when she saw her. Lola was not close to Tunde's mother, but she didn't expect that kind of reaction from her, Lola enquired about Tunde. His mother said, she has just woken up and does not know where he is. Lola called his phone again, again, no answer. Lola told his mother of the death of her father, Tunde's mother sympathy towards the news of Lola's father's death seemed genuine. Tunde came round an hour later to show his respect and to talk about the funeral arrangements. He apologised to Lola; he made up an excuse about his phone falling into water, Tunde claimed he left the phone outside to dry. They finished discussing the funeral arrangements, and they agreed to come back down in three days' time. Lola told the driver to drive back to Lagos, she is going back to Lagos with her husband. Lola wished her mother farewell and left with Tunde to his mother's house.

When they got there, Dupe was in the kitchen cooking. Tunde's mother had that same look of agitation on her face. Lola could also tell that Tunde was uncomfortable with Dupe being there. Dupe stood at the door with attitude written all over her face. Lola knew right there and then that Tunde was having an affair with Dupe. Tunde ignored Dupe and picked up his bag and got in the car with Lola. Lola left the house without even saying goodbye to Tunde's mother. Tunde's mother didn't make a big deal about Lola's rudeness because she had a guilty conscience.

Lola decided not to speak to her husband about their marriage; she now believes her husband had moved on. Lola asked her husband why Dupe was at his mother's house, he gave her some excuse about Dupe being close to his mother; Dupe has been helping her since she had no one else. 'If your mother had someone cooking and cleaning for her, how come you have spent so much time in Ibadan?' Asked Lola. 'I have spent so much time in Ibadan because I am moving back there, my mother needs me,' replied Tunde. He told Lola that, he does not want his mother to rely too much on strangers. 'Have you arranged all this without discussing it with me?' Asked Lola. 'You have been grieving the loss of your child; I didn't want to give you any additional stress,' replied Tunde. 'I have been grieving the loss of our child,' Lola shouted at him. Lola then asked her husband where her and Temi fitted into his plans? Tunde was quiet for a while; then he said you and Temi can join me later when the business is up and running. They drove in silence for the rest of the journey home, Lola knew her marriage was over. Dupe's mother had cursed her many years ago, she said then that, Lola would never find happiness. For the first time in a while, she thought about Wale; she was wondering if her life would have turned out differently if she had joined Wale in America.

The following day there was a knock at the door, it was the police; they had a warrant to search the house. Lola was panicking because the police wouldn't tell her what they were looking for, they searched the house and turned everything upside down. They didn't find what they were looking for and left. Lola tried to call Tunde and could not get hold of him. She called the manager; he answered the phone and then hung up on her. Lola told the driver to take her to her husband's office. According to the secretary, Tunde was arrested over some business transaction, the secretary didn't have all the details. All she knew was that the police came from Lekki Police stations. Lola rushed to Lekki police station, they confirmed that her husband was there, but wouldn't tell her anything else, and they wouldn't let her see him. Lola was in such a state of confusion and didn't know what to do, she felt faint; she had only four hours sleep in two days. It was all taking its toll, she had no choice but to call Alhaji. Alhaji was on his way if anyone could sort this out he could. Alhaji arrived and asked to speak to the divisional police officer. The divisional police officer came out of his office when he realised who was asking for him. Other low-ranking officers referred to him has the DPO. The DPO rushed both Alhaji and Lola into his office, he read out all the charges against Tunde. Lola said it couldn't be true; there was no need for her husband to embezzle money, she refused to believe it. The DPO showed Lola and Alhaji all the paperwork and cheques, he had signed for the fraudulent transactions. Lola recognised the documents; she told Alhaji and the DPO that, her husband's manager had brought the documents to the house for him to sign. Her husband must have been signing the documents and cheques without reading them. The DPO looked at Lola with a disapproving eye. Alhaji asked the DPO if Tunde has been interrogated about this and he said he had. The DPO said he had signed the documents and cheques without reading them. Alhaji requested that they release Tunde pending the investigation. Tunde walked into the DPO office; he was relieved to see his wife and Alhaji. He knew Alhaji was the only one that could get him out of this mess. The police had beaten him, hoping to get a confession out of him. Tunde pleaded with the DPO to send the police to go looking for his manager. Tunde could not leave Lagos until the investigation was over. Alhaji took both Lola and Tunde home. They concluded that Alhaji and his wife would attend Lola's father's funeral, while Tunde stayed behind. Alhaji dropped Lola and Tunde off at their house. He promised to call them in the morning. Lola went straight to bed, she was so exhausted, due to the lack of sleep. For the first time in ages, she longed for her husband's presence. He curled up beside her and held her tight until she fell asleep.

Alhaji and his wife came to pick up Lola. Lola kissed her husband on the lips, he is upset he couldn't attend his father-in-law's funeral. They had pleaded with the DPO to let him go to Ibadan for the funeral. The DPO said it was impossible; it was only due to the influence of Alhaji that, he was not behind bars. The following day Tunde received a call from the DPO to come to the police station, Tunde arrived at the police station. They had arrested the manager at the airport with most of the money he had stolen from Tunde's business partners. Tunde had signed cheques for over fifty million. The Police recovered thirty million of the money from the manager. According to the manager, he had spent twenty million of the money trying to secure his visa and property in the US. When the DPO asked why he had embezzled the money from his employer, his only excuse was that Tunde didn't care about the business and left him to do everything. Tunde's Business associates wanted to know, who would pay the remaining twenty million that the manager had already spent. The DPO told Tunde that he had to pay the twenty million back to his business associates, they cannot be penalised for his negligence. Tunde would have to sell his business to raise the money. The DPO said he would have to pay his business associates or go to prison with his manager, his business associates agreed to drop the charges if Tunde reimbursed them.

The funeral was a quiet one; only close friends and family attended, they all agreed to have a celebration of life in a months' time. Lola stayed with her mother for two days and returned to Lagos with Alhaji two days later. Lola's mother would join them in Lagos after the celebration of life. Lola didn't want to leave her mother in Ibadan but, her mother had to stay because of all the well-wishers coming to pay their condolence.

Chapter Five

The relationship between Lola and Tunde was getting back on track, he was so appreciative because Lola stood by him during his time of need. He knew deep down he still loved her and couldn't live without her; he decided that he would call off the relationship with Dupe. Tunde took out a loan and used the business as collateral; he used the money from the loan to pay off his business associates. Tunde used the rest of the money he got from the loan to start a small business in Ibadan. Tunde was spending more time in Ibadan, this time he had a good enough reason to do so. The business in Ibadan was doing well, he had made a lot of business contacts from the business he had in Lagos to support the business in Ibadan. Tunde had people working for him, but he was cautious with all business transactions. It was a case of once bitten, twice shy, he would work in Ibadan during the week and return to Lagos every weekend to see his wife. He called her every day, sometimes three to four times a day. Lola loved the attention she was now getting from her husband.

Dupe arrived at Tunde's office as he was about to leave, he had been ignoring her calls. Dupe told Tunde twelve weeks ago that she was pregnant, and he is the father. He told her to get rid of it because he would not leave his wife for her. Dupe went to see Tunde's mother and told her she was carrying Tunde's baby, but he wants her to abort the baby. Tunde's mother told Dupe not to worry she will speak to her son. Dupe was not happy to wait; it wasn't her intention to have a child for Tunde, she only wanted to ruin the relationship between him and Lola. His mother went to the local hospital to find out what Dupe's genotype was, her friend works at the general hospital as a nurse, as soon as she confirmed Dupe's genotype was AA, she put her plan into action. Dupe's genotype is AA and Tunde's genotype is AS; they could only ever have a baby with or without the sickle cell trait. Tunde's mother did not want to leave anything to chance, she knew Lola would never forgive her for not telling her about Tunde's father having sickle cell anaemia and for keeping it a secret from her own son. Lola had cut Tunde's mother off from her only grandson, she was glad when Dupe told her she was pregnant with Tunde's child. Tunde's mother pleaded with Dupe to keep the child; she promised Dupe that, Tunde would marry her. Tunde's mother tried to convince Tunde to accept Dupe's baby, she tried emotional blackmail; she even told Tunde that she would kill herself if he did not listen to her, out of anger he told his mother to carry out her threat because he would never accept the baby.

'Tunde, why have you been ignoring my calls?' Asked Dupe. 'I have been busy;' he replied. 'This baby is not going away; don't you think it's time we sat down and talked about the future of our child?' Dupe cried, 'how can you treat me this way? Four months ago, you were telling me you want to be with me forever;' she said. Tunde replied, 'I love my wife, I won't jeopardise our marriage for your sake.' Dupe was furious, 'I will not get rid of this baby,' she shouted. Tunde was trying to keep her quiet. 'Don't hush me, I want everyone to hear I am four months pregnant with your child,' she shouted. Tunde's phone rang; he looked at the phone, Lola's name flashed up, he knew he could not answer the phone. Lola had complained about him not answering the phone when she rang in the past, he knew he had to get rid of Dupe, so he could ring his wife back. 'Is that your useless wife on the phone?' She shouted out. Tunde turned around and gave her a slap across the face. Dupe took a few seconds to compose herself. 'How dare you slap me because of that witch that only gives you children that die?' Tunde saw red; he was just about to slap her again, his phone ringing distracted him, so Dupe slapped him instead. Tunde grabbed her and he was shaking her about like a rag doll. Dupe was shouting and screaming. 'He is trying to kill my baby;' she kept yelling. The people in the office were standing in the doorway pleading with their boss to leave her alone. Tunde stopped, shaking her. Dupe was sobbing, 'how can you hate me so much? What have I done to deserve this treatment from you?' She kept repeating the same questions over and over again. By this time Tunde had calmed down, he told her to go home, he will follow behind her in his car, so they could talk in private. 'You have been avoiding me for weeks why should I believe you now?' She asked. He said he was sorry for what he had put her through and promised to drive behind her. Dupe hesitated, Tunde then suggested that they both drove in his car. Dupe said no, she needs to be in Ore first thing in the morning and that she will need her car. They both left the office together, as soon as Tunde got in the car, he played Lola's message on his phone. Tunde turned his car around, missing the car coming in the opposite direction. Dupe noticed him turn in her rear mirror and followed him. 'This man is playing games with me, he will see my true colours today,' she said. Tunde headed to his mother's house; when he got there, he jumped out of the car and told his mother he must go back to Lagos right now. Lola had fallen down the stairs at work, she is at the hospital, he tried to call her back, but the phone went to voicemail. He tried his mother-in-law's number but; she didn't answer. Tunde went into the house and took his things; then he jumped into his car. His mother was trying to stop him but, he wouldn't listen to her. Dupe drove up, she was shouting at the top of her lungs. Tunde told them both that he had to go back to Lagos, Lola is in the hospital. Tunde's mother shouted at him. 'Is that why you want to kill yourself?' She didn't want to show concern for Lola in front of Dupe. Tunde's mother came closer to the car so that Dupe couldn't hear her and asked Tunde if Lola would be okay? 'How the hell do I know when I am here,' he replied. Tunde's mother pleaded with her son to calm down, you have a two-hour drive to Lagos, she wanted to go with him; he said he didn't have time to wait for her to get ready. Dupe was standing next to Tunde's mother; she was still crying and not happy that

Tunde was ignoring her. He promised to come back and see her. ‘When are you coming back?’ Asked Dupe. ‘I am not sure, I will call you tomorrow,’ replied Tunde. His mother cradled Dupe in her arms and promised her that, Tunde would call her tomorrow and If he didn’t, she will take her to Lagos, he gave his mother a disapproving look, but he shook his head in agreement. He pulled Dupe towards him and told her he loved her, and she should wait for him to get back, he promised her that everything would be all right and bid them both farewell. Tunde drove off with so many things running through his mind. How is he going to explain Dupe pregnancy to Lola? He didn’t want Lola to find out from anyone else. All along, he hoped that Dupe would end the pregnancy, he didn’t understand why Dupe was insisting on keeping the baby; he knew his mother had something to do with it. Dupe had threatened so many times to tell Lola. Tunde had to decide what he would do; he knew Lola would leave him if she found out. He weighed up his options in his mind, after the birth of Temi, Lola told him she would not have any more children with him. The thought of having another child with sickle cell anaemia would kill her. Tunde agreed with her but, he secretly wanted a big family. He was the only child of his mother, he had a half-sister, who lived with her mother. Lola's business was doing well in Lagos; Tunde had asked Lola to move back to Ibadan so, he could get his own business up and running. Lola refused, she was not willing to move back to Ibadan and leave her business. In Tunde mind, he was looking for someone to blame for his infidelity, he blamed Lola for pushing him into the hands of Dupe. Tunde did not feel guilty about having a baby outside his marriage; he wished the baby's mother was someone else. 'Why did I tell Dupe I loved her?' He asked himself. He didn't love her; his mother was the one that engineered the relationship from the start. His mother made sure that Dupe was around every time he was in town. Tunde decided that when he returns to Ibadan, he will buy a plot of land to build his own house. He rang his mother-in-law again; Lola's mother didn't answer her phone. Lola's mother knew all about the affair with Dupe; she was ignoring his calls. Lola called Tunde again, Tunde put her on loudspeaker to talk to her. 'Are you on your way?' Asked Lola. 'Yes, I am,' replied Tunde. She told him she has seen the doctor and her arm is not broken, but, she must wear a sling, I will need help with Temi. Lola didn't want her mother to know because she is still mourning. Tunde told her not to worry, he will be in Lagos soon. 'I have been trying to call your mother, have you spoken to her?' Asked Tunde. 'No, I haven't spoken to her yet, I don't want her to worry about us,' replied Lola. 'Okay, if she calls me back, I will just tell her I was calling to let her know I was on my way to Lagos,' replied Tunde. 'Good Idea, let me get off the phone as you are driving, drive safely and call me as soon as you get to Lekki.' Lola said. 'Will do,' replied Tunde. He thought about telling Lola about Dupe pregnancy, he didn't want his marriage to be over because of Dupe and his unborn child but, he didn't want Temi to be his only child either. It would have been much easier to explain to Lola if Dupe was not the mother of his unborn child. The only consolation in all this mess was that his child would not have sickle cell anaemia. Tunde's mother had told him that, she had checked Dupe's genotype, and she has the AA genotype, that pleased him. The text message interrupted his thoughts, he picked up the phone to read the text message. The message was from Dupe; I am so sorry I slapped you, I don't know what came over me. I can't wait for you to get back. Love you always. Signed D with a love heart. He was just about to text her back when he looked up from the phone; it was too late to react to the lorry driver from the opposite side, who had tried to overtake the car in front, smashed head-on into Tunde's car. Tunde died at the scene.

It was now almost three hours since Lola spoke to Tunde, he should have been here by now. Lola called his mobile again but, it rang out. Lola called Alhaji's wife and told her she is at the hospital with her baby, she also told Alhaji's wife, she could not get hold of Tunde. Alhaji went to the hospital to pick Lola and Temi up, he took them to his house. He had his suspicions where Tunde might be but, he kept his thoughts to himself, he didn't want to upset Lola.
Alhaji knew of the affair Tunde was having with Dupe, he had even confronted Tunde about the affair, Tunde told him to mind his own business. Alhaji threatened to tell Lola if he didn't put a stop to the relationship with Dupe. 'Yes, you would love that, wouldn't you? You would then have my wife all to yourself,' said Tunde. Alhaji walked out of Tunde's office after calling him an ingrate and vowed never to speak to him again.

Lola fell asleep; the pain relief given to her made her drowsy, she woke up an hour later to the sound of her baby crying; he looked so much like Babatunde, she fed Temi, then they both fell asleep again.

In the morning, Lola called her mother and asked her to call Tunde's mother, Lola didn't want to speak to her. Lola's mother told Lola that Tunde had called her several times yesterday evening. 'Why didn't you answer your phone?' Asked Lola. Lola's mother had to think about her response before answering, I left my phone in the bedroom; I didn't see the missed calls until now. 'Why was he calling me?' Asked Lola's mother. 'I fell down the stairs at work; I hurt my arm, he called to tell you,' replied Lola. 'Why didn't you call me?' Asked Lola's mother. 'I didn't want to worry you, I am okay, I have got to wear this sling for a while,' replied Lola. Lola told her mother that Tunde was on his way back to Lagos to help with Temi. 'I will call Tunde's mother now and find out if he is still in Ibadan,' said Lola's mother. 'Okay, please call me back after you have spoken with Tunde's mother,' said Lola. 'I will,' replied Lola's mother. Tunde's mother was frantic over the phone. 'Tunde left for Lagos yesterday evening,' she shouted down the phone. Lola's mother could tell that Tunde's mother was telling the truth, Lola's mother thought he was lying to Lola when he told her he was on his way to Lagos, she thought he was spending the night with Dupe. Lola's mother called Alhaji and asked him to make sure Lola stayed with them; she's convinced Tunde was in an accident, and that is why no one has heard from him. Alhaji asked Lola's mother if anyone had spoken to Dupe? 'Alhaji, why did you ask me that?' Asked Lola's mother. 'Before we all jump to conclusions, talk to Dupe first, I am sure Tunde's mother knows how to get in touch with her,' said Alhaji. 'Okay,' replied Lola's mother. She was so relieved that she was not the only one keeping this dirty secret from her daughter. Lola's mother called Tunde's mother again and asked if she has seen Dupe, Tunde's mother said yes, we are both going to the police station. Lola's mother said she would meet them there. Tunde's mother went to the police to report her son missing; the police told her that there was an accident yesterday evening, the police told them to go to Ore, they would have information of the persons involved in the accident. Tunde's mother was crying; she had a terrible feeling it was her son; he had left yesterday in such a state. She asked Dupe, to accompany her to Ore. Lola's mother arrived at the police station. Tunde's mother was sobbing; Lola's mother couldn't understand what she was saying. Dupe told Lola's mother that, there was an accident at Ore. Dupe was talking to Lola's mother, but, Lola's mothers was staring at Dupe stomach. Dupe asked Lola's mother if she wanted to go with them to Ore? Lola's mother said no. Lola's mother had every intention of going with them to Ore until she realised that Dupe was pregnant. Lola's mother was finding it very difficult to compose herself, she knew this was not the time or the place to bring up her pregnancy. Lola's mother got back into her car and called Alhaji to give him the latest update. She told Alhaji that Dupe is pregnant and that she can no longer keep Dupe and Tunde's affair from Lola. Dupe is so desperate to flaunt her relationship with Tunde; she doesn't care who knows. Alhaji said, he didn't know Dupe was pregnant, all he knew was that Tunde was having an affair with her and he was trying to call it off, now it makes sense why he wanted to call the affair off. Alhaji thought it was because he threatened to tell Lola. 'The accident at Ore, was it fatal?' Asked Alhaji. 'The police officer said, no one survived,' replied Lola's mother.

Tunde's mother and Dupe arrived at the police station, the car registration confirmed that the Mercedes Benz belongs to Tunde. The police asked them to go to the local mortuary to identify the body. The grief was overwhelming for Tunde's mother; she could not enter the room. Dupe ended up going into the cold room to identify the body, she also had to sign the paperwork. Dupe had flashbacks from when her husband died, 'there must be something wrong with me, how can this be happening again?' she whispered to herself. She hadn't realised that she had signed the paperwork has the next of kin, she also paid part of the bill for the cold room. They both drove back to Tunde's mother's house, Lola's mother called Tunde's mother; Dupe answered the phone. 'Let me speak to Tunde's mother,' insisted Lola's mother. 'She won't talk to anyone,' replied Dupe. 'Give her the phone for Christ's sake.' Dupe put the phone to Tunde's mother's ear. Lola's mother was trying to talk to her, but, Tunde's mother was inaudible, she kept shouting out that her dear son has left her, she put the phone down because Tunde's mother was not making any sense. Lola's mother took a taxi to Tunde's mother's house; she waited for them outside the house.

Tunde's mother arrived about thirty minutes later she, was still crying for her son. Lola's mother tried to comfort her. The neighbours also came over after hearing Tunde's mother screaming. They all went into the house. Lola's mother felt so sorry for her, the worst thing that can happen to any parent, is the loss of their child. Lola's mother cradled Tunde's mother in her arms and was telling her to take heart. Tunde's mother was not listening; all she could do was cry. Lola's mother was thinking about her daughter, how is she going to take this news of her husband's death? Lola is still very vulnerable; she has only just come to terms with the death of her baby and her father. They haven't even completed the burial ceremony of her father yet, this was all too much for them to bear why was God punishing them? 'What have we done Oh Lord?' asked Lola's mother.

Quite a few people in the town had heard about the death of Tunde; they were coming to offer their condolences. Dupe was feeling out of place as no one seemed to notice she was in the room. Dupe went over to Lola's mother to tell her that, she was going home. Lola's mother looked at her with so much disgust in her eyes. 'Why are you telling me? I couldn't care less if you are here or not, to be honest, you have no business being here, you witch, it wouldn't surprise me if all this, is your doing, get lost,' Lola's mother shouted at her. 'How dare you shout at me? No matter what you think of me, Tunde loved me, and I am carrying his baby, 'replied Dupe and stormed off when she realised that everyone was looking at her. Tunde's mother was crying and rolling on the floor.

Alhaji and his wife had to break the news of Tunde's death to Lola. Lola fainted as soon as they told her, they had to rush her to the hospital. The doctor gave her a sedative to calm her down, Lola woke up after what seemed like an eternity. Alhaji and his wife were both sitting at her bedside with Temi. 'Where is my husband?' She asked them. 'Lola, he died in a car crash,' replied Alhaji. 'No way, that's not possible, he can't be dead, I haven't finished burying my father yet, and now you want me to bury my husband,' Lola said. I can't do this; someone has put a curse on me.' Lola remembered the words of Dupe; Dupe told her years ago that she would never find happiness. Lola was looking for someone to blame for her misfortune. 'Alhaji, I believe Dupe has something to do with all the terrible things happening,' Lola said.

‘What made you say that?’ Asked Alhaji. ‘She was having an affair with my husband,’ replied Lola. ‘Who told you that?’ Asked Alhaji. ‘I know, my husband was acting strange, and she was always hanging around Tunde’s mother’s house. I know something was going on but, I had no solid evidence to prove it.’ Lola said. Alhaji looked at his wife; Lola caught the look Alhaji’s wife gave him. ‘You both know something, don’t you?’ Asked Lola. ‘Don’t be silly Lola; this is not the time to be talking about Dupe, you have just lost your husband let’s concentrate on that,’ Alhaji pleaded with her. Lola felt alone, she tried so hard to hide her disappointment from Alhaji but, she couldn’t understand why they kept Tunde’s affair from her. She was wondering if her mother knew, she was always so hostile towards Tunde. Lola decided that she would have it out with Tunde’s mother, she hated the woman. Lola asked the doctor to discharge her, she told the doctor she was feeling okay and that she needed to go home and grieve for her husband. Alhaji didn’t want the doctor to discharge Lola, but, he had no reason to keep her in the hospital. Alhaji asked Lola to come back to their house but, Lola refused, ‘I don’t want to appear rude but, I want to be alone, and please respect my wishes.’ He dropped Lola off at home; Lola didn't even want Alhaji to come in. Alhaji looked worried, he didn't want to leave her alone. 'If you need anything, please call me, 'Alhaji said. 'I promise you; I am okay, I will call you if I need you,' replied Lola. Alhaji drove off promising to call her the next day even if she didn't call him. Lola gave him a reassuring smile and waved him off, she was sitting in the kitchen feeding Temi, Temi looked so much like his father. She sat and cried, she didn't want to believe she would never see Tunde again. After feeding Temi, she put him in his cot. She had so much to do, but she didn't know where to start. Lola dialled her mother's number; she will tell her what to do. Lola's phone rang, it was Abbey Tunde's younger sister.

Abbey is an attractive girl, Abbey loved the attention that came with dating a socialite. Abbey and Ade attended the funeral of Babatunde, during the wake-keeping, one mourner told Ade that, Babatunde died of sickle cell anaemia. Two weeks later Ade told Abbey that, he has booked an appointment for her to do a genotype test. He wanted to know if she had inherited the sickle cell gene. Unknown to Abbey, Ade has the sickle cell gene. Ade told her he would not marry her if she has the sickle cell trait. 'I thought you loved me?' Asked Abbey. He responded by saying he loves her so much, but he doesn't want to bury any of his children. Abbey wanted to know why he was treating her like a leper. 'What have you to hide? It's a simple request, your brother's child died of sickle cell anaemia only three weeks ago. Unless you want all my kids to die of the same blood disease, you will take the test, if you don't want to take the test you need to leave my house,' said Ade. 'I thought it was our house?' Asked Abbey. 'Make sure you are not here when I get back, you are an evil woman; you tried to charm me with your beauty, I am a socialite, a man of the world, I know your sort, you are planning to ruin my life. Well, you have failed, make sure you are not here when I get back, or I will kill you and take your dead body to your parent's house,' Ade said all of that without coming up for air. Abbey drove to Ade's mother's house to tell her what had happened. Ade's mother likes Abbey and always stuck up for her when Ade did anything wrong. Ade's mother knows Ade has the trait. This time she could not stick up for Abbey, she had already lost one child to sickle cell anaemia. She insisted that Abbey should take the test and that everything will be okay if she doesn't have the sickle cell trait. 'I will only take the test if Ade takes it too,' said Abbey. Ade's mother responded by telling Abbey to leave her house. I will not allow you to insult me in my house. Abbey left Ade's mother's house and that same day she moved out of Ade house. Abbey was finding it difficult to believe her five years' relationship with Ade ended over something so ridiculous. The break-up was in all the gossip magazines. The magazines even went further to say she was having an affair, and that was the reason Ade broke up with her. Abbey called Ade to tell him to stop spreading malicious rumours about her. Ade just responded by telling her never to call him again; he also said, she has seen nothing yet, and that he has just got started. The following week the magazine posted that, Abbey had sickle cell anaemia, and she had tried to hide the fact from her intended husband. Abbey is angry; she ended up taking the test for her own peace of mind, she knew she didn't have sickle cell anaemia; the results proved that her blood type is AA. She took a long time to get over Ade, but the constant pictures in the magazines of him with different women helped turn her love for him into hate and then much later it turned into pity. Ade got married to a high society lady, she was beautiful, very tall, fair-skinned and very wealthy. Even though she had done the genotype test at his request, she had the results falsified. Ade's wife had gone to see a spiritualist who had told her not to worry since her husband didn't have the sickle cell gene, he will make her sickle cell gene go away. Nine months later she gave birth to her first son after six weeks the doctor confirmed that their child has sickle cell anaemia. There was a rumour going around that Abbey blamed Tunde and Lola for the break-up of her relationship with Ade. Lola had always suspected that Tunde's mother had spread that rumour because she was envious of how close Tunde and Abbey were. Abbey was Tunde's half-sister. Tunde's father had an affair with Abbey's mother. Abbey's mother knew Tunde's father had sickle cell anaemia and that, he wanted no more children after having Tunde. Abbey's mother was a gold-digger, and she hoped that she could snatch Tunde's father away from Tunde's mother by having his child. It didn't work, Tunde's father wanted nothing more to do with Abbey's mother but, he sent an allowance for his daughter. Abbey went to live with her grandmother because Abbey's mother didn't want to bring Abbey up has a single parent and she was a constant reminder of her relationship with Tunde's father. Tunde's father had a good relationship with his daughter; she would always come and spend the school holidays at her father's house. Tunde and Abbey shared a close bond that displeased Tunde's mother. Tunde's mother called Abbey and told her about the death of Tunde; she couldn't believe Tunde has gone so soon. Lola and Abbey talked and cried for ages over the phone. She apologised to Lola for not keeping in touch with her since the death of Babatunde. Abbey told her it wasn't intentional, the longer she stayed away, the harder it was for her to make contact, she said she knows she can't compare the loss of a child to a break-up with a boyfriend but, she needed time on her own, she also said she wasn't in the right frame of mind and Tunde was always the person she could go to when she was feeling down but, he had just lost his son so, she dealt with her own demons on her own. Lola told her she understood what she was going through but, they were a little disappointed because she blamed her break-up with Ade on them. Abbey said she didn't blame them for her break-up and that she didn't understand why they would think she blamed them. According to Lola, Tunde's mother implied that abbey blamed them for the break-up. Abbey said Tunde's mother can be so vindictive sometimes and she was adamant she never blamed them for her break-up with Ade. The ignorance surrounding sickle cell anaemia is an epidemic, it shouldn't take a tragedy to make people act. The lies Ade spread in the magazines about her having sickle cell anaemia, got people talking about the blood disorder and it made many people get tested. Ade's ignorance created awareness about the blood disorder. Lola agreed with Abbey about Ade creating awareness for sickle cell anaemia without him knowing. 'What are you going to do now?' Asked Abbey. 'I was just about to call my mother before you called, I need to go to the mortuary in Ore and get Tunde transferred to Ibadan,' replied Lola 'I am on my way over now, I will go with you, you can't go alone,' Abbey said. 'Thank you so much, Abbey, I will appreciate the company.'

Lola called her mother to let her know she was on her way to Ore and that she would bring Tunde's body back to Ibadan, her mother said it's not a good idea for her to go alone. Lola told her mother she is not alone that, she is going with Abbey, Tunde's sister. 'Okay, please let me know when you arrive in Ibadan, I am still at Tunde's mother's house,' said Lola's mother. 'How is she doing?' Asked Lola. 'Not so good, she has been crying nonstop, she will make herself sick,' replied Lola's mother. The doctor is here; he will give her a sedative to calm her down.' Lola understood what she was going through; she knew what it felt like to lose a child. Lola called her driver and told him they are going to Ore and then onto Ibadan. Lola and Abbey set off for Ore, Lola had mixed emotions; she didn't know if she wanted to see her husband's body or if she wanted to remember him the way he was, she cried. Abbey tried to comfort her at the back of the car. 'Save your tears my darling; you need to be strong,' Abbey said. Lola was just about to thank Abbey for being there for her when a police officer knocked on the driver's car window and asked in broken English. 'Where your particulars? Wetin dey for boot?' The policeman kept asking all these questions without letting the driver answer any of them, he got out of the car to speak with the police officer. The driver got back in the car, and they were soon on their way again. Lola was in deep thought; she was reminiscing about the happier days, well before the birth of Babatunde, they were very much in love and inseparable. Every lunchtime, Lola would cook for Tunde and take it to his office. Their lunch breaks could go on for hours; Tunde would always say Lola was distracting him. Lola would respond same time tomorrow my love, he would smile, even though she was distracting him, he loved it. Lola had a smile on her face, the cry of her baby brought her back to reality. Abbey interrupted Lola deep in thought as she passed Temi to her to feed him, she took her baby and gave Abbey a disapproving look. Abbey ignored her; she didn't want to distress her any further. Abbey knew what it's like to lose the one person you love. Abbey was also grieving for her brother, but she wanted to stay strong for Lola.

Lola's mother is thinking about how she will tell Lola about the affair between Tunde and Dupe, keeping the dirty secret was bad enough, finding out she is pregnant was adding salt to the injury, she would have to tell her as soon as she arrives in Ibadan, she didn't want Lola to find out from anyone else. Lola was suffering from postnatal depression after the birth of Temi, there was no way Lola could have handled the news of her husband having an affair with Dupe of all people. Lola's mother had gone to Tunde's mother's house to confront her. The rumour was that Tunde's mother had encouraged the affair, both women argued if not for Tunde's presence the argument would have turned physical. Lola's mother had no choice but to agree not to tell Lola about the affair just yet. Tunde wanted to be the one who told Lola. Dupe walked in at that moment, it surprised her to see Lola's mother there. Lola's mother hailed abuse at her, she called Dupe a slut and a husband snatcher. Dupe responded with the usual arrogance in her voice. 'I did not snatch Lola's husband; she let him go.' Lola's mother had heard enough and walked out. Tunde ran out after her to apologise. 'What are you apologising for? You made your bed, so you will lie in it.' 'Tunde, you don't deserve my daughter, you and Dupe deserve each other, I hope and pray that she leaves you when she finds out.' Tunde's mother was standing at the door with Dupe, she shouted over to Lola's mother and said she doesn't care if Lola leaves her son. I want a wife that can give my son children without diseases. Lola's mother cursed back, nothing good will come out of this relationship, mark my words. Then she got into the car and told her driver to drive off.

Lola and Abbey arrived at the hospital at noon. They went straight to the mortuary to see her husband. As soon as Lola got to the door, she became hysterical. 'Oh my God, what have I done to deserve all this heartache?' A gentleman walked up to Lola and asked her to follow him into the room. Lola was weeping; she was inconsolable. Lola was asking God why he allowed this to happen to her. Tunde looked so peaceful, Lola kissed his forehead and told him to sleep well. Lola also prayed for God to forgive him his sins. Abbey was with her as soon as she saw her brother lying on the table, she cried. They stayed in the room for about fifteen minutes holding each other's hand. Abbey then led Lola away. Lola had to sign the paperwork to release Tunde's body and make the final payment. Lola was standing in the doorway, waiting for the driver of the ambulance that, would take her husband's body to Ibadan. It was raining, and she didn't want to stand in the rain. Lola was waiting near the entrance door, the lady at the reception desk was shouting out the name of Ms Ogunlana. A young boy ran over to Lola and said, in broken English 'Madam dem dey call you.' Lola was surprised that the lady was referring to her. Lola heard her shout out, but she didn't think she was shouting over to her. Lola went over to the reception desk; 'my name is not Ms Ogunlana why did you call me that?' The lady responded. 'You signed your name as Ms

Ogunlana the other day.' Lola asked to see the paperwork. Lola couldn't believe her eyes, Dupe had signed the paperwork and paid the first instalment. Lola screamed for Abbey to come over, she shoved the paperwork in Abbey's hand. Lola was so angry; she shouted at the woman at the desk, so, 'do you mean to tell me, anyone can come in here claim a body if they have the money to pay?' The lady at the desk looked so confused. 'I need to call the manager; I only deal with the paperwork.' The woman in reception called for the manager, when the manager got to the reception area, he spoke to the woman at the reception desk and then he walked over to Lola. The manager was an arrogant man, and he was talking in broken English. Lola was wondering how such a weasel got the position has a manager. 'Wetin happen?' Asked the manager. Lola looked at him from head to toe, she was just about to give him what for, but Abbey stepped forward. 'The person who signed the paperwork is not the next of kin why did you allow this woman to sign the paperwork?' Asked Abbey. 'Madam, no vex, na the mama for sign, but she been dey cry too much so the wife sign. As she carry belle, I think say she be the wife. I dey wonder why she no sign Mrs Adewale,' replied the manager. Lola

shouted at the manager; 'she is not his wife that is why she didn't sign has Mrs Adewale, I am his wife.' The manager looked confused, 'him mama say she be him wife so, the man get two wives, it no matter who sign na.' Lola wanted to slap his face, but Abbey pulled her away. Lola tried to pull away from Abbey to carry on arguing with the manager. 'Just because the woman was pregnant that, does not make her the next of kin,' said Lola? 'Madam, the woman sign on behalf of her mother-in-law and the mother-in-law confirmed that she was the dead man's wife,' replied the manager. 'Mother-in-law,' Lola repeated. Abbey pulled Lola away and asked her 'who is Ms Ogunlana?' 'Ms Ogunlana is the woman who has been having an affair with your brother and now I have just found out she is pregnant, I know your brother is the father of her unborn child,' replied Lola. 'This is unbearable; I am grieving for a man who had no regards for me.' Abbey is in shock, she knew Tunde's mother could be callous, but, she didn't think she could be so heartless. Lola instructed
the ambulance to take Tunde's body to the mortuary in Ibadan, she decided not to follow in the ambulance. Lola was going straight to Tunde's mother's house to have it out with her. Abbey was trying to discourage her from doing

that, everyone knows about Tunde and Dupe relationship and the fact that Dupe is having a baby made Lola sick to her stomach. ‘I am not weak, just because I had a breakdown after the death of my son Babatunde, everyone thinks I will fall to pieces. My son’s death strengthened me,’ Lola said. Tunde’s mother and Dupe can bury Tunde and she will not waste her tears anymore. She would have gone back to Lagos but, she needs to see her mother, she knows her mother knows of Tunde’s affair, it makes sense now, she was always hostile towards him. Lola told Abbey, her father would be the last person she will grieve for. Abbey was begging Lola to take it easy and calm down, ‘I know he is your brother Abbey but, no one makes a fool out of me, all the signs were there; I ignored them,’ Lola said.

Lola and Abbey arrived at Tunde’s mother’s house; the house was full of mourner and well-wishers. Lola was ready for a showdown; she was looking around the room for Dupe. Abbey ran over to Lola’s mother and told her what Lola had just found out. She pleaded with Lola’s mother to stop Lola from doing something she might regret. Before Lola’s mother could get up from where she was sitting, Lola was shouting at

Tunde's mother. 'Look at you, sitting on the ground whaling like an animal; anyone would think butter wouldn't melt in your mouth. This is just the start of your sorrows, wicked people like you will always reap what they sow.' Everyone in the room looked stunned and confused; they didn't know what she was talking about, two ladies rushed over to Lola to calm her down, they thought she was grieving for her husband. 'You and Dupe are welcome to each other; I will not grieve for your son. Only God knows what his plan was for me,' Lola said. Tunde's mother was sobbing and asking for forgiveness. Lola's mother with the help of the two
other ladies persuaded Lola to go outside, as they led Lola out of the house, Lola looked back over her shoulder at Tunde's mother and told her that, her son is in the mortuary and that she and Dupe can do what they please with him.

'Mother, how long have you been keeping Tunde's dirty secret?' Asked Lola. 'My daughter, I found out three months ago;
I confronted Tunde and his mother, I
demanded that Tunde should tell you or I will tell you myself,' replied Lola's mother. 'Why didn't you tell me?' Asked Lola. 'I wanted to tell you my daughter; I was thinking about your

health. You were recovering from postnatal depression and I didn't want to stress you any further by telling you about your husband's infidelity, I insisted that Tunde told you, it was my belief he would have told you before the unfortunate accident happened.' Lola took her baby of her mother and walked off towards the car. Lola's mother jumped into the car too. 'I am sorry you had to find out about Tunde and Dupe the way you did,' Lola's mother said. 'It was horrible mother, the manager at the mortuary told me, he didn't even realise I didn't have a clue.' Lola said the most annoying thing is if Tunde didn't die in the car crash, he would have left me anyway. Her mother told her she didn't think he would have, he had tried to end it with Dupe many times, he didn't love Dupe, it was his mother that engineered it all. Lola said they will never know what Tunde would have done and besides, her mother never gave her the opportunity to find out. She blamed her mother for not telling her about the affair. Lola said she would have had it out with him but, she will not worry myself about it now, 'you are all expecting me to fall apart and fall back into a deep depression, but, I am a mother and a superb businesswoman, I will let nothing or anyone stand in my way again.'

‘Good for you Lola, but, you will still need to grieve for your husband,’ said Lola’s mother. 'I am not grieving for Tunde; I will get on with the rest of my life.’ Lola replied. They sat in silence for the rest of the journey home, she was so angry that she never got the chance to have it out with Tunde, her marriage was one big lie. Both their parents wanted them to get married, she wanted to be with Wale.

Lola called Alhaji and told him about the affair between Tunde and Dupe; she needed his advice. Since her father died, he was the only one she could turn to and trusted. He told her to attend the funeral as normal, not to say anything to Tunde’s mother or Dupe. Alhaji told her she will flaunt the pregnancy in your face, but she should play ignorant. He told her it will be hard, but she needs to attend her husband’s funeral if only for the sake of her family. Lola didn’t want to attend, but Alhaji convinced her to attend. People can be evil; they will turn around and say you killed your husband. They will say you found out about Tunde’s new wife and killed him. Alhaji and his wife arrived that evening; they booked into a hotel close by to Lola’s mother’s house. They will stay in Ibadan for two weeks, to make sure that Lola didn’t do or say anything she would live to regret. Lola had to stay in Ibadan for forty days to mourn her husband. Alhaji and his wife stayed for as long as they could, they didn't want Lola left alone with Tunde's side of the family. Alhaji had various businesses in Ibadan, so he conducted his business from Ibadan to keep an eye on her. His wife was with Lola every day for two weeks. Tunde's mother had turned up at Lola's mother's house several times. Everyone pretended as if nothing was wrong. Lola found it difficult to hide her true feelings. They would talk about the preparations for the funerals. Tunde's mother made most of the preparation regarding her son's burial, only close family and friends would attend because Tunde died so young. Lola was still hurting, she couldn't get Tunde's betrayal out of her head, she wanted the burial over and done with. On the day of the burial, everything went to plan; it was a beautiful send off for Tunde. Dupe being at the funeral didn't ruin it for Lola. Dupe tried to make herself so relevant, but Lola just ignored her. The after-party went on all night, Lola made her excuses and left early, leaving Dupe to take over playing the hostess. Lola noticed that she didn't see Dupe cry at the funeral and she thought it was strange, Lola cried, but she wasn't crying for Tunde she was crying because of the pain he had put her through. For the next two weeks, people were coming to the house to pay their respect. The night before Alhaji and his wife was to go back to Lagos; he went to see Lola. Alhaji told her he has been checking up on Tunde's business affairs, he told Lola that although the business was doing well, Tunde owed the bank a lot of money. Alhaji said she might have to sell the business to pay the bank loan off unless she wants to keep the business going herself. That means, she would have to move back to Ibadan, even though her business is doing well in Lagos, she had no intentions of moving to Ibadan. Lola told Alhaji that she would sell the business to pay off the bank. I want nothing to do with his business dealings she said.

A week later Tunde's mother and Dupe turned up at Lola's mother's house. Lola was trying so hard to keep her composure. Tunde's mother demanded the paperwork for the business, she needed to make sure that Dupe's child gets his inheritance, Tunde is the father of Dupe's baby. Tunde's mother was waiting for Lola to react. Lola told her to go to the office and speak with the manager, he has all the paperwork. Lola told

Tunde's mother she wants nothing to do with Tunde's business. Tunde's mother was not satisfied with that response, she wanted Lola to give her power of attorney for all Tunde's business dealings and accounts. Dupe was shouting and screaming that Lola had taken everything in Lagos. Lola had to remind her that Tunde had no investments in Lagos and that he invested everything here in Ibadan for her and her baby. I am sure your mother-in-law can testify to that, so please leave me in peace. Lola's mother then shouted back at Dupe; Lola is Tunde's wife; you were just his bit on the side. Dupe screamed that's a big lie, I was not his bit on the side, he would have left Lola and married me. Lola just saw red; she wanted to take her frustration out on someone and Dupe was the perfect candidate. Lola slapped Dupe across the face; that gave Lola so much pleasure. Dupe tried to slap her back, but, Tunde's mother stood in front of Lola. Tunde's mother said to Dupe, calm down my daughter. 'Don't let her make you lose this child.' Lola shouted, 'she better get out of this house and take her unborn bastard child with her. I am wondering why all her baby fathers end up dead.' 'Lola, you are the most vicious bitch, I know,' replied Dupe. Dupe walked out of the house trying to hold back her tears. Tunde’s mother turned to Lola and said, ‘you better not fight me for Tunde’s business.’ ‘You can have his business; it’s not worth anything, I need nothing from your son, I will look after my child. Now can you both leave my mother’s house?’ shouted Lola. Tunde’s mother and Dupe let and Lola was hoping she didn’t have to see them ever again. Lola’s mother was so disappointed with Lola’s behaviour towards Dupe and Tunde’s mother; she wasn’t happy that Lola brought herself down to their level. Lola apologised to her mother for losing her temper, but, she didn’t regret her actions.

Chapter Six

Three years later Lola's mother bumped into Tunde's mother at the Yaba market in Lagos. Tunde's mother had aged so much; her hypertension had gotten worse. Mama Lola, she called out to her. 'How are you? How is Lola and my grandson?' Asked Tunde's mother. 'They are both doing well,' said Lola's mother. How are you asked Lola's mother? 'My health is failing, I came to receive treatment at the Lagos teaching hospital; I am staying with Abbey; I miss my son so much; he would never have let me suffer like this,' she had tears in her eyes. Lola's mother felt sorry for her, even after all she had put her daughter through, she couldn't help but show compassion towards her. 'What about Dupe and your grandson? Does she not help you?' Asked Lola's mother. 'Dupe is a disappointment, she sold my son's business and moved away; I haven't seen her since. Abbey sends me money, but she is not my daughter so, I cannot expect too much from her. I am all alone and no one cares about me. Please ask your daughter to forgive me,' said Tunde's mother.

Dupe took over the ownership of Tunde's business, she had sold her own business and invested in Tunde's business. She found out that the old accountant is Alhaji's nephew so; she got rid of him. The new accountant didn't know about the the loan secured on the business. Tunde had taken out a loan to pay off his previous partners in Lagos and used the business as collateral, the previous accountant knew this but; he didn't inform Dupe or the new accountant. If Dupe had known about the loan, she would have negotiated with the bank for more time. Dupe had received a call from the manager to come to the office. The manager told her she had visitors from the bank and they need to talk to her about a loan. The manager told her he believes it would be in her best interest if she met with the bank officials as they are requesting to see the new CEO in person. If they wanted to see me, they should have booked an appointment. Dupe was doing her hair; she was getting impatient with the manager. 'You are the manager, so manage,' she shouted. The meeting took place without Dupe. The bank officials were furious that Dupe refused to meet with them. Dupe even turned down the offer of a conference call. The bank officials gave Dupe two weeks to pay back the investment loan, or they would close the business. The manager knew this was not just a threat, after the meeting, he left several messages on Dupe's voice message for an urgent callback. Dupe did not call him back, so he went to her house and told her about the meeting. Dupe couldn't believe the previous accountant kept this vital information from her, he had done this on purpose because she sacked him, she now must come up with thirty-five million in two weeks. Even though the business was doing well, there was a limited cash flow. The next day she met with the company lawyer. He gave her three options; she would have to come up with thirty-five million or sell the business or plead to the bank for more time. Dupe tried to meet with the bank manager but, he refused to see her after the way she treated his bank officials when they tried to meet with her. She had no choice but to sell the business but where would she find a buyer within two weeks.

Dupe received a mysterious phone call from the accountant; she had sacked; he was offering to buy her out. 'Where will you get the money to buy me out?' Asked Dupe. 'That's none of your business,' he replied. 'How dare you speak to me with that tone of voice?' You are just a common accountant and not a good one at that,' replied Dupe. 'Are you willing to sell or not?' Asked the accountant. 'Yes, I will sell for twenty million.' Dupe responded. 'I will pay you five million,' the accountant replied. 'The business is worth over sixty million,' snapped Dupe. 'It's worth nothing if you can't pay off the bank loan,' replied the accountant. 'Why didn't you tell me about the bank loan?' Asked Dupe? 'I was under no obligation to tell you anything,' replied the accountant. 'You removed the paperwork from my office,' said Dupe. 'I did not; the paperwork was always in my possession, if you hired a reputable accountant, he would have realised that Tunde has a thirty-five million deficit. The bank gave Tunde a year to pay off the loan. Tunde's wife is aware he took out a loan; she was a signatory to the loan. It's obvious that Tunde had no regards for you, if he did, you would have known everything about his business. You can take the five million or leave it, it's your choice. This way you walk away with five million, I will take over Tunde's business' he replied. Sleep on it and let me know what you decide. I am staying at the hotel across the road, room three thirteen.' Then he ended the call. He was relying on Dupe's greed to accept the deal.

Dupe took the paperwork to Tunde's mother; she was the only one that can sign the business over to the accountant. Dupe told Tunde's mother she was selling the business as it was failing. 'How much are you selling it for?' Asked Tunde's mother. 'Twenty million,' Dupe replied. Tunde's mother was so surprised; 'I didn't think it was worth that much; he owes a lot of money to the bank,' she replied. 'So, you knew about the loan? Why didn't you tell me about the loan?' Asked

Dupe. 'I thought you knew,' replied Tunde's mother. 'It was common knowledge he borrowed money to pay off his former business partners in Lagos, give me the paperwork, let me sign it before the person changes their mind.' Tunde's mother signed the paperwork giving Dupe the power of attorney to sell her son's business. I will see you tomorrow, said Dupe. Dupe had no intention of seeing her ever again.

Lola's business was doing well in Lagos; she wanted nothing to do with Tunde's business in Ibadan. Tunde's former accountant was Alhaji's nephew, Alhaji instructed the accountant to pay off the bank loan and open a trust fund for Dupe's son. Dupe's son could take over the business when he is twenty-one, no one told Dupe about Alhaji's goodwill gesture for her son. Dupe's son is an innocent child and had nothing to do with the wrongdoings of his mother or father. Alhaji spoke to Lola about running the business until Dupe's son was old enough to run it himself. Lola re-confirmed that she wanted nothing to do with the business and that she had no problem with Dupe's son inheriting the business or money from it. She loved Alhaji even more due to his thoughtfulness. Alhaji's nephew paid Five million into Dupe's account, she moved to Lagos and that was the last time anyone heard from her.

Alhaji arranged a conference call with Lola and one of his business contacts, the contact is the owner of an Italian fashion house in London; they wanted her to move to London and run the African fashion side of the business. African prints have become so fashionable and it's big business. Lola called Alhaji about the business proposal. Alhaji told her to take the job; she could start a new life in the UK, it's a great business opportunity. 'What about my business in Lagos?' She asked. 'You can run both businesses,' Alhaji replied. After speaking to Alhaji, he convinced her that going international would help her business in Lagos. With the technology, we have today; it's possible to have the best of both worlds. The plan was for Lola to go to London on her own, so she could find a place to live. A hotel room was not an ideal place for Temi or her mother to stay in. It was an emotional send-off, Temi was crying, he didn't want his mother to leave him. Lola wanted to buy a plane ticket for him, Alhaji put an end to that idea. 'You can't take him with you now; it's not practical, are you going to take Temi to all your business meetings? I will call my friend's son and ask him to look for a house for you to buy,' said Alhaji. 'Don't worry my daughter, I will look after Temi, he will be okay with me,' said Lola's mother. Lola bid them all farewell. Lola could not eat on the plane; she felt guilty, she had convinced herself that, leaving her son behind was the wrong thing to do. By the time she arrived in London, she was an emotional wreck and starving. Alhaji's friend's son Mark is an Estate Agent, he met Lola at the terminal three arrivals; she told him she wanted to rent a flat right away. 'I thought you wanted to buy a house?' Asked Mark. 'Yes, I do, whichever one is quicker, my mother and son need to join me as soon as possible,' said Lola. 'It's eight o'clock in the evening, we will talk about getting you an apartment in the morning,' said Mark. Mark took her to the Hilton hotel on Edgware Road, it is a very nice hotel. Lola checked in and she and Mark went up to her room. Lola ordered from the room service menu, thirty minutes later room service knocked on the door with her food, Mark left and promised to come and pick her up in the morning. She was not even halfway through her meal; she fell asleep. Lola woke up three hours later, it was past midnight. Lola called her mother; her mother wasn't asleep; she had been waiting for her to call. 'Mother, how are you? How's my son? I hope he is well?' Asked Lola. 'My daughter, how many questions do you want me to answer at the same time?' Lola apologised. 'Temi is okay, and he is asleep,' she replied. 'I am so sorry it's late, but I fell asleep,' said Lola. Her mother told her not to worry; the fact she arrived safely is all that matters. Lola said she would call first thing in the morning to speak to Temi, she bid her mother Goodnight. She felt much better after talking to her mother. Lola called room service to come and take away the half-eaten food, and she got ready for bed, she has an early start in the morning.

Chapter Seven

Lola woke up at six in the morning; she called her mother, she can hear Temi singing his favourite song in the background, who's in the garden, a little fine boy. Lola's mother gave the phone to Temi, Temi had so much to tell her, she was just listening to his voice, not paying attention to what he is saying, she missed him so much, this was the longest time spent away from her son. Lola asked Temi to give the phone back to grandma, and she promised to talk to him again when he gets back from the nursery. She spoke to her mother for a little while and then got ready to meet Mark in the lobby of the hotel. Mark was downstairs in the lobby waiting for her; one thing Lola had to learn is that time waits for no one. African time is not acceptable in the UK. They arrived late to the meeting at the fashion house; the traffic was atrocious. The CEO had left for breakfast with another fashion designer who had flown in from Italy. Lola had to wait for two hours before they returned. Mark and Lola had breakfast at the restaurant in the fashion house. The CEO of the fashion house is a tall, dark, handsome Italian man, he was angry that she arrived late, and he instructed the receptionist to make his feelings known to her. It didn’t take him two hours to eat his breakfast, but he made it a point to punish her by making her wait for him. 'Hello Lola, my name is Mr Goite,' he said. Lola apologised for arriving late. Mr Goite told her not to make it a habit, most Nigerians have difficulty with timekeeping. 'The traffic is atrocious in London, but you must make allowances for that, in the fashion business, keeping your client’s waiting is unacceptable,' replied Stefan. Lola felt like a little school girl being told off by the teacher, in her mind, she was thinking if he has dealt with Nigerians as he claims he has, he would know we don’t like being spoken to in such a manner. Lola didn’t appreciate being stereotyped, Mark caught her expression, Mark knew she was about to say something, he shook his head. Lola got the message and smiled. Mr Goite noticed the silent discussion between Lola and Mark, so he changed the subject and introduced his client from Italy. This is Mr Galiona; he is the personal designer for one of our British celebrities; he is in town for the London fashion week. Mark excused himself; he needed to find a flat for Lola. The driver is in reception waiting to take Mr Galiona off to the West End to watch a fashion show; he is a special guest of one of the top designers. Lola and Mr Goite went into his office to talk about her contract with the fashion house. 'Please call me Stefan; I know we got off on the wrong foot; I am a nice guy really.' Lola sat in silence; she had already made her mind up about him. Lola didn't like Stefan; she wasn't often wrong about people. 'My name is Lola,' she responded. 'I know who you are; you have an excellent reputation in the fashion industry;' he replied. Lola smiled, she wasn't aware that her reputation had reached all the way to London. They talked about the three-year contract the fashion house has with Nollywood; she was to oversee all the costumes the stars would be wearing. They talked about travelling expenses, salary, and accommodation. Lola was well pleased when she realised the job came with a beautiful four bedrooms flat in Marble Arch. Lola signed the contracts and the lease to the apartment. Stefan asked if he could take her to dinner, Lola said not today because she will be busy moving into the new apartment. Stefan asked her what she was moving into the apartment because the apartment is furnished. Lola then lied and said Mark is taking her to dinner, he smiled but said nothing. They concluded their meeting, Lola went to sit in the reception area; she has had enough of Stefan's wit for one day. Lola called Mark to come and pick her up, he is stuck in the rush hour traffic and he wasn’t moving, he told Lola that he would be there in one hour. After an hour, Lola called Mark again; he hadn’t moved from the last time she called him. There must be an accident, Lola is getting frustrated; she didn’t want Stefan to come out and still see her sitting there. Lola went over to the receptionist, to see if she could direct her back to her hotel, she knew the name of the hotel but, she didn't know the location. At that moment Stefan came out of his office. 'Are you still here? I thought you left hours ago.' Asked Stefan. 'I am waiting for Mark; he is coming to pick me up; ' Lola replied. Stefan offered to take her back to the hotel, Lola declined his offer and told him it won't be necessary; she will wait for Mark. Stefan told her that the office is closing in one hour, he asked her how long is Mark going to be? Lola said she didn't know so Stefan asked her to call Mark, so she could find how much longer it would take him to get to the office. Mark was trying to explain to Lola where he was and how long he thinks he might be. Stefan asked Lola if he could speak to Mark, she gave him the phone. After the phone call, Stefan decided it would be much easier for him to take Lola to the hotel and then to Marble Arch where the flat was. The police had closed part of the M1 due to an accident; he had gone to look at an apartment in Hemel Hempstead for a client. Lola had no choice but to accept the kind offer from Stefan. He took her to the hotel; she packed her things, and he paid for the hotel room. Stefan then took her to the apartment in Marble Arch. 'Lola, you need groceries, let me take you to Waitrose so you can buy what you need?' Lola saw a different side to Stefan, he thought of everything. After she had bought the things she needed at Waitrose, Stefan asked her again, if he could take her to dinner? Lola agreed this time, he had helped her settle into the apartment, the least she could do was to allow him to take her to dinner and she couldn't come up with a good enough excuse to say no. Stefan said he would come and pick her up at eight o'clock. Lola was glad when Stefan left; it gave her the opportunity to have a good look round the apartment. The apartment is beautiful; it had a lovely balcony; the rooms are nice and big, and the kitchen was massive. There wasn't a garden for Temi to play in, but she noticed the massive park across the road as they drove up to the apartment, it was just five minutes away. Lola called Mark to find out if he got home okay since he didn't have to go to the West End anymore, he got off the M1 at the next junction and took the back roads to Harrow where he lived. Lola told Mark that he no longer needed to find her a flat that the job came with an apartment. After she finished speaking to Mark, she called her mother and told her; she has an apartment and that both her and Temi can come over, they both agreed that they would wait until the summer; it would give Temi and her mother time to get used to the cold winters. Lola had already decided that she would return to Lagos in December, so she could celebrate Temi birthday and Christmas.

Lola had spent so much time talking to Temi on the phone, he was just talking to her about anything that came into his head; she loved hearing his voice. Temi was the only good thing left from her relationship with Tunde. Lola asked Temi to give the phone to his grandma, Temi said goodbye to his mother. Lola's mother came on the phone. 'I will call you tomorrow; I must get ready now, I am having dinner with my boss,' said Lola. 'That's nice,' her mother replied. It's not a date Lola was quick to remind her; Lola's mother wasn't convinced. 'My daughter tell me all about it in the morning.' 'I have nothing to tell,' replied Lola. 'Okay, my dear, I will speak to you tomorrow.' Lola had been chatting away on the phone; she had lost track of the time. It was now seven thirty, she only had thirty minutes to get ready. Lola remembered how horrible Stefan was when she was late this morning, she jumped in the shower for a quick one as she got out of the shower; she heard the doorbell. 'Oh, my God, Stefan is here already,' she felt embarrassed as she went to open the front door wrapped in a towel. Lola apologised for not being ready, she told him she lost track of time talking on the phone to her son. Stefan was too busy eying her up and told her not to worry that a gentleman does not mind being kept waiting by a beautiful woman for pleasure, she blushed and then she remembered she was talking to Stefan in her towel half-naked; she excused herself. Lola got ready; she put on her little black dress. Lola always looks good in the clothes she wears, she knew her body type and always dressed according to her body shape. As soon as she stepped out of her bedroom, Stefan couldn't help but stare. Lola had to clear her throat to get his attention. 'You look stunning in that dress; you could pass for a model,' he said.

Stefan took Lola to an Italian restaurant; it was such a lovely place in Soho, Lola found out later the restaurant belonged to his brother. The food was delicious after eating; they sat and talked and got to know more about each other. Stefan divorced his wife of twenty-three years, according to Stefan, his wife ran off with a younger man. It was at the time he was building his empire so; he was paying less and less attention to his family. Even though he blames himself for his wife infidelity, he has refused to take her back after the younger man broke off the affair. The younger man was only interested in the security he thought Stefan's wife could offer him. Stefan remained cordial with her for the twin's sake, he had twin teenage boys. Lola told Stefan about her tragic life in Nigeria, she had never told the story to anyone before; she surprised herself by talking about her life story with Stefan. The restaurant belongs to Stefan's brother so; they didn't have to leave after their meal. They sat and talked for ages. Lola warmed to him, I guess I was wrong about this man; she thought to herself. It was getting late, so they both left the restaurant, they had an early start in the morning. Stefan is taking Lola to meet the supplier of the African fabrics to the fashion house. Stefan drove up to her flat entrance and walked her to the door, 'do you want me to come up?' he Asked. 'No,' Lola said. Lola noticed the disappointment on his face so she said it's late and we both have an early start in the morning. He smiled and asked if he could kiss her; she didn’t answer, so he kissed her on the lips. She pulled away, but she liked it. 'Goodnight Stefan, thank you for a lovely evening.' 'Did you enjoy my company?' Asked Stefan. 'Yes, I did,' Lola replied. 'Can we do it again soon?' Asked Stefan. 'I think we should keep our relationship professional,' replied Lola. 'As you wish,' replied Stefan. He said Goodnight and walked back to his car, he was furious, how dare she make me feel this way. Lola lay on her bed thinking about Stefan; she couldn’t believe she allowed Stefan to kiss her and worse of all she enjoyed it. Lola decided that she will keep her distance from Stefan; it would not be easy as they work together, she needed to find out the route to work and back; she doesn’t want to rely on Stefan. 'I will call Mark in the morning, he will show her how to get around London,' she was thinking out loud. Lola got off the bed, got undressed and went for a shower. After her shower, she put on her pyjamas; she had the sudden urge to call her mother; she glanced at the time; it was after midnight. 'It’s too late to call now, I will call in the morning,' she thought to herself.

Lola had set the alarm clock at six o'clock in the morning; Stefan was coming to pick her up at nine o'clock. She didn't want to be late. The one thing Stefan hates is people who keep him waiting. Lola called her mother; her mother wanted to know everything about the date. 'How was the date? Did he kiss you? Do you like him?' Asked Lola's mother without letting her answer any of her questions. 'How many questions do you want me to answer at the same time?' Replied Lola. Lola's mother ignored her sarcastic tone. 'Do you like him?' Lola mother asked again. 'Yes, he is a nice guy.' replied Lola. 'What did you talk about?' Asked Lola's mother. 'We talked about lots of things, mainly business,' replied Lola. 'Are you keeping things from your mother? If it all goes wrong, just remember you refused to talk about it. Your mother knows best.' 'Okay, mother,' can I speak to Temi now?' Lola's mother shouted over to Temi, come and speak to your mother. Temi got on the phone and wanted to know why she didn't call him yesterday, she was just about to answer his question but; he interrupted her and told her about his friend next door; they had a falling out over a toy. Lola listened and asked him to make up with his friend, she told him falling out over a toy is silly. Temi said he will talk to him at school today. Lola told Temi to give the phone to grandma and to get ready for school. 'What are you doing today?' Lola's mother asked? 'I am going with my boss to meet a supplier,' Lola replied. 'You are spending a lot of time with your boss; I hope there's nothing to it?' Lola's mother asked. 'I have got to get ready for work, I will call you later. Bye, mother,' and she disconnected the phone. Lola wanted to tell her mother everything, but she was not sure how she was feeling. Lola didn't want to feel the way she did about Stefan.

Stefan arrived dead at nine o'clock; he rang the doorbell. Lola shouted down the intercom for him to come on up, Stefan said he will wait in the car. His tone sounded serious, Lola grabbed her handbag and locked the door behind her. Lola didn't want Stefan to think she was not ready. The driver opened the car door. 'Good Morning, Lola,' said Stefan. 'Good Morning Stefan,' she replied. Stefan was quiet for the fifteen minutes' drive to the office. When they got to the office, Stefan told Lola that they are going to the suppliers at eleven o'clock and he asked if she has had her breakfast? Lola said no, Lola didn't understand why he was so cold towards her. Let's have breakfast first, then we can head off to East London. Lola said she was not hungry that he could have breakfast without her. He looked at her and walked off towards the fashion house restaurant. Lola was hungry, but she would not let Stefan treat her like a child. Lola went over to the receptionist and asked where she could get a sandwich; the receptionist told her that Macdonald's was across the road. Lola went to Macdonald's and had a McDonald's breakfast, she called Mark while she was enjoying her breakfast. 'Mark, when am I going to see you?' She asked. I can come to the apartment this evening, text me your address and I will come and see you after work.' Mark replied. Mark said he will see her later; he was just about to get into his car. 'See you later,' replied Lola.

Mark's father and Alhaji used to be business partners. Mark's father met Mark's mother while he was on business in London. They had an affair, and it lasted for three years, she ended it when Mark's father refused to leave his wife for her. Mark's mother never told Mark's father she was pregnant with his child, Mark would often question his mother about his father, she refused to talk about him. When Mark was eighteen, he threatened to leave home if she didn't tell him how to get in touch with his father. She had no choice but to give him Alhaji's contact details. Alhaji knew about the affair but, he didn't know about Mark. It was Alhaji that informed Mark about his father's recent death. Mark's mother carried the guilt of not telling Mark's father he had a son. After finding out about the death of Mark's father; she refused to leave the house; she blamed herself for not giving her son the opportunity to have a relationship with his father. The guilt was the start of her depression. Mark's mother still lives with her mental illness, she is not getting any better, she has been on anti-depression pills for over five years. Mark is a workaholic; he is always on the go, the business is very lucrative, but Mark takes too much on, he has had too many failed relationships because he can't commit to relationships. Mark has a four-year-old daughter, her mother is from the Caribbean, St Lucia to be exact. She broke up with him, because she wanted to get married, but he wasn't ready. Alhaji told Mark to look after Lola while she was in the UK, he even told Mark that Lola is wife material. Ever since Mark's father died, Alhaji has taken on the role of Mark's father. As soon as Mark saw Lola, he liked her; Mark knew Lola liked him too. Mark wanted Lola to rely on him as much as possible;

he wasn’t happy that Stefan had taken an interest in Lola; Mark wanted to make sure she spent less time with Stefan; he didn’t trust him with Lola. Italian men have this mentality that Nigerian women are easy to manipulate.

Lola returned to the fashion house after enjoying her McDonald’s breakfast, Stefan was talking to the receptionist. Lola could tell he knew where she had been. 'I thought you weren’t hungry; he asked?' 'I changed my mind,' Lola replied. 'Well, that is a woman’s prerogative, 'he said. Lola didn’t understand what he meant by that, and she didn’t like the tone of his voice either. Stefan was being facetious. 'If you are ready, it’s time to meet the supplier.' Stefan said. 'I am ready; ' she replied. He smiled at her, but she ignored him. They drove to East London in silence, they got to Liverpool Street; the driver drove round to find a parking space while Lola and Stefan walked through the market, the number of textile shops in Liverpool Street market surprised Lola. Stefan and Lola walked to the textile shop at the corner of Liverpool Street. They walked through the shop to the back office. Stefan knocked on the office door and a voice said come in. A lady called Bisi was the shop owner and the supplier for the fashion house. She jumped up from her seat and threw her arms around Stefan and kissed him on both cheeks. Bisi kept flirting and asking Stefan inappropriate questions. It was so obvious to Lola that; they are an item. Stefan felt uneasy and Bisi sensed it and looked toward Lola. 'Hello,' Bisi said with an attitude. 'My name is Bisi,' she said, without even looking at Lola. 'My name is Lola,' she replied. Bisi asked them both to sit down. Bisi asked them what they wanted to drink. Lola said she didn't what anything to drink. Bisi looked over at Stefan, she was flirting with him and asked if he wanted his usual? Stefan said yes, sheepishly. Stefan and Bisi were talking to each other, it felt as if they had forgotten she was in the room. After about ten minutes of being ignored, Lola asked Stefan, 'how much longer will he be?' Bisi replied, 'my dear, are we boring you?' Lola was so angry at this point. Lola asked herself, 'how dare she talk down at me in that tone of voice? She is of no use to the business; she is probably ripping the fashion house off.' 'I am not bored, I am meeting my boyfriend later; I need to know what time to tell him to meet me,' replied Lola. Bisi found pleasure in that response; she thought Lola was taking her place in Stefan's life. Stefan looked shocked, Lola glanced at him; he looked upset. Stefan took a sip of the wine he was drinking and told Bisi it was time for them to leave, he didn't want to stand in the way of true love. Bisi and Stefan laughed at his joke, Lola was trying so hard to fight back the tears. They bid Bisi goodbye, Bisi told Stefan not to be a stranger and slapped Stefan's bottom. Lola could feel the rage brewing inside her, Lola couldn't understand why she was feeling this way? Lola wanted to slap Bisi, but she managed a smile and stepped out of the shop. Stefan and Lola were walking towards the parked car and the driver. Stefan asked Lola why she didn't tell him that Mark is her boyfriend? Lola replied that she didn't think she had to give him an account of her personal life. 'You are a tease; why did you allow me to kiss you last night?' Asked Stefan. 'I didn't, you took advantage of me,' replied Lola. 'How dare you, what are you accusing me off here?' Shouted Stefan. 'I am not accusing you of anything, all I am saying is that you shouldn't have kissed me,' replied Lola. 'Why are you being like this?' Asked Stefan. 'Like what?' Replied Lola. 'Forget it; I don't like arrogant people.' 'Who are you calling arrogant? Have you told me about all the women in your life, like Bisi for example?' Stefan ignored the question, and they both remained silent for the rest of the walk to the car. When Stefan got to

the car, he instructed the driver to take Lola where ever she wanted to go and he took a cab home. He left without saying goodbye to Lola. Lola was so angry; she was having trouble holding back the tears. 'Why was he so rude?' I need to get a grip; he is my boss.' She wanted to call him to apologise but, she was unsure what she was apologising for. Mark's name flashed up on her phone. 'Hello Mark, how are you?' Lola asked. 'I am fine my dear, how are you?' Mark replied. It was so nice to hear a friendly voice, he always knows the right things to say, he has never been abrupt or arrogant towards her. Lola was in deep thought; she wasn't listening to what Mark was saying. 'Are you listening?'
Asked Mark. 'Yes, I am,' Lola replied. I am on my way to your apartment, are you home yet? I will be there soon, she asked her driver how long it would take for her to get home; he said twenty minutes.

The driver dropped her off, and she went straight to the kitchen, Mark said he fancied jollof rice and plantain with chicken. Mark rang the doorbell, Lola let him in, she had just finished preparing the meal. She laid the table, and they both sat at the dinner table and talked about their day. Lola didn't tell Mark about her argument with Stefan. 'It's been a long time since I have had a good meal cooked for me, I could get used to this,' said Mark. 'I am glad you enjoyed your meal,' replied Lola. 'I loved it, said Mark. Lola cleared the table and put the dishes in the dishwasher, she took out a bottle of red wine from the fridge and went to join Mark in the living room.

Stefan got home, he was so angry with himself for leaving Lola, he couldn't get over the fact that Lola was dating Mark. 'Why did she keep that from me?' he asked himself. Stefan called Lola to apologise for his bad behaviour, he knew he acted like a jealous schoolboy. He called Lola's phone; she answered. 'Hello Lola, how are you?' He asked. 'I am fine; how can I help you, Stefan?' She asked. 'There is no need to be like that, I wanted to make sure you got home okay,' he replied. 'Well, thanks for asking I did,' she replied. 'I see you are not in the mood to speak so I will call you tomorrow, replied Stefan. Mark's phone rang; he was speaking on the phone. I see you have company?' Asked Stefan. 'Yes, I have Mark came over for dinner, Lola replied. 'Okay, let me not keep you. Goodbye,' he put the phone down without letting her reply. Stefan was furious at himself, for letting Lola get to him. He went to his drinks cabinet and took out a bottle of Moet and drank it. I will teach that woman a lesson. The last time I felt this way, was when I found out my wife was having an affair. He finished the bottle of Moet; he was so drunk, and he ended up throwing up, Stefan had not got so drunk in a long time, his head was pounding, he lay on his bed, dressed and he fell asleep. In the morning, he had a terrible hangover; he called the office and told his personal assistant he does not want to speak to anyone and told her to cancel all his meetings, even the one he had with Lola. Stefan wasn't seen in the office all week. Lola called Stefan on Wednesday; she wanted to know if the meeting scheduled for the afternoon with Bisi is still going ahead. Stefan's phone went to voicemail, she left an urgent message for a callback. He never returned her call. Lola was getting fed up with Stefan's behaviour, he was acting like a child. Lola was just about to call Stefan again but her phone was ringing, it was a call from Nigeria. She answered the phone; it was her designer. 'Hello madam, how are you?' he asked. 'I am fine,' Lola replied. How are you and the family? 'What can I do for you?' Asked Lola. The designer called to give her some good news; the Minister in Benin wants us to design the outfits for his daughter's wedding. 'That's fantastic news,' Lola said. The Minister's wife wants Lola to order the materials, and she wanted Lola to call her urgently, I have texted you her number. Lola told him she will call him as soon as she puts the phone down, she thanked him for calling. Lola called the Minister's wife; she asked Lola to go to Switzerland to buy her material; she wanted no expense spared. Lola told her she would go to Switzerland to see her manufacturer, to make sure she gets the latest designs in lace and print materials. No one would have access to the same material until after the wedding. Lola booked a flight to Switzerland; she would go first thing tomorrow morning and come back the same day. She called Stefan and left a message letting him know she will not be in the office tomorrow. Lola's phone rang, Mark's name flashed up on her phone, she was hoping it was Stefan returning her call. 'Hello, my darling, how are you?' He asked. 'I am okay, how are you?' She replied. 'I am fine too; I have no more appointments this afternoon. Do you want to go for lunch?' Asked Mark. 'I can't, I am going to Switzerland tomorrow morning; I need to make sure I complete my schedule before I leave. I could not get hold of Stefan, and I don't want to give him an excuse to have a go at me, for some unknown reason, he is being evasive.' replied Lola. 'I understand, book a seat for me, I haven't been to Switzerland, we can have lunch over in Switzerland,' said Mark. 'Okay, that's a date, come and pick me up later tonight, it will be easier to get to Heathrow Airport from your house,' replied Lola. 'Good idea, I will see you later,' replied Mark.

Lola and Mark were getting closer and closer, Mark treated her like a Queen. Lola knew she could talk to Mark about anything. Mark rang the doorbell, Lola let him in, she had just finished cooking yam porridge. Mark loved Lola's cooking, anytime he planned to eat at Lola's apartment; he would starve himself all day. 'Lola, yet again you have outdone yourself, the yam porridge was delicious,' he said. 'Thank you,' Lola replied. Lola went into her bedroom to get her hand luggage. Mark joined her in the bedroom; he kissed Lola all over her neck, he then turned her towards him and kissed her on the lips. Lola kissed him back, she felt aroused. Mark whispered in her ear, I want to make love to you. Lola was like putty in his arms, she had not felt like this in a long time. Mark unzipped her dress and let it drop to the floor. Lola was just standing in her bra and panties. Mark took off his shirt, still kissing her, he wiggled out of his jeans and boxers, he then laid Lola on the bed and kissed her again. Lola's bra opened from the front, exposing her breast. He caressed her breast; then he sucked on her nipples. Lola had her eyes closed; she already climaxed with his touch. Mark then put his hand down her panties, she was wet. Mark knew it was time to take her to ecstasy. He took her panties off and he was inside her with ease. Lola was groaning, they both climaxed, she could feel herself shaking, she moved away from Mark, but he pulled her back and held her close to him until he fell asleep. Lola was wide awake; she was ashamed of herself for letting Mark seduce her. This relationship can't go anywhere until she knows his genotype, she knew she had to talk to him about it, the past can never repeat itself. Lola worried herself to sleep; she woke up because Mark was caressing her breast, they made love again, and then they both fell asleep in each other's arms. Lola woke up, it was three o'clock in the morning. Mark was lying beside her still asleep. They had to be at the Airport at noon, the plan was to leave from Mark's house, but, they never made it to his house. Lola set the alarm clock for seven in the morning and went back to sleep.

The alarm went off, Lola got up and went to the bathroom to brush her teeth. The shower was running, after brushing her teeth, she got into the walk-in shower. Mark shouted to her 'Good Morning, my love.' 'Good Morning, Mark,' she replied. 'I need a toothbrush,' he shouted. 'look in the cupboard under the sink,' she replied. Mark brushed his teeth when he had finished, he got into the shower with Lola. He was caressing her again. Lola said stop it; we need to get to the Airport on time, we've no time for this. We have loads of time; he grabbed hold of her and pulled her towards him, she kissed him and got out of the shower. 'You tease,' he shouted. Lola ignored him. Lola was in the kitchen making tea and toast, Mark joined her in the kitchen and sat at the dining table. 'Do you want scrambled eggs or boiled eggs with your toast?' Asked Lola. 'I will have whatever you're having,' Mark replied. 'Boiled eggs then,' she said.

They drove to the Airport and left the car in the Airport car park, there was no time for them to get to Mark's house and call a taxi to the Airport. Mark called his mother, to make sure she was all right, she was expecting them home last night. When they arrived in Switzerland, the manufacturer was waiting at the Airport to meet them. The manufacturer drove them to the factory, to have a look at the samples he had reserved for them. Lola loved them and placed her order. Something else had caught her eye. Bisi had shown them a sample of lace she wanted to supply to the fashion house, she told Stefan that, the fashion house would be the first people to have the lace, but her manufacturer was producing the same material for someone else and at a much cheaper price. Lola's manufacturer told her that, he has orders for two separate customers, he also said the sample is so popular amongst his customers. Lola asked to see the paperwork for the orders, one of them was Bisi's order, she asked if the sample was brand new, the manufacturer said no, it had been in circulation for a while now, she asked to see more samples, the supplier showed Lola another lace; it was brand new and not in circulation yet. Lola liked it better than the one Bisi had chosen and it was much cheaper, Bisi had also inflated the price. Lola called Stefan to tell him what she had discovered; she left him a message to say she will cancel Bisi's order and he should get back to her by the end of tomorrow if he is not happy with her decision. Lola called Bisi and cancelled her order, anyway. Bisi was so angry, 'you stupid bitch, who do you think you are? You have no authority to cancel my order, I will call Stefan,' she said. 'I have already cancelled your order, I will deal with the suppliers from now on, we no longer need your services,' replied Lola. 'Who the hell are you? You are a stupid cow; I have been supplying the fashion house for years,' Bisi said. 'Thanks for that but, your contract has ended, and I have taken the decision not to renew it,' said Lola. 'If the contract has expired, it's an oversight, Stefan will deal with this issue,' replied Bisi. 'Don't you ever call me again,' Bisi disconnected the call. Lola was feeling proud of herself, she had gotten one over Bisi. 'That will teach her to mess with me,' she said out loud. 'That was so unprofessional, why did you have that conversation with Bisi over the phone? You could have arranged a meeting to discuss your findings,' said Mark. 'This has nothing to do with you; I know how to conduct my business. The woman has been robbing the company for over two years. I have seen the books, I will not let her get away with it anymore, not on my watch,' replied Lola. 'Lose the attitude, do you think Stefan doesn't know the woman has been ripping him off, for all you know, he is having it off with her, and so he doesn’t care?' said Mark. 'I don’t care what you think. I have a three-year contract with the fashion house, and I will not let a low life hussy rip off the business,' replied Lola. Mark had struck a nerve when he said Bisi might be having it off with Stefan. Lola already suspects they are or were having an affair. 'Are we going to lunch now?' Asked Mark. 'I think we should head back to the Airport; we can catch an earlier flight, I am no longer in the mood,' replied Lola. 'What is wrong with you? It’s not your business, why are you taking it to heart?' Asked Mark. 'Can we stop talking about this now; I don’t interfere with your business, so why are you interfering with mine?' Asked Lola. Lola called for a taxi; they drove back to the Airport in silence. That was their first fight.

Mark and Lola arrived in London; they hadn’t said a word to each other since they left Switzerland. Mark drove Lola home in complete silence. When they arrived outside the flat, Lola asked Mark if he wanted to come in for something to eat, he said no thanks, he would speak to her soon. Lola is feeling sorry for herself, she shouldn’t have taken her frustration out on Mark. Mark has been nothing but kind to her and she knows what he said was true. Lola decided that she will wait till he get home, then she will call him to apologise. Lola's phone rang, Mark's name flashed up. 'Hello Mark, I am sorry about the way I spoke to you. I was out of order; please forgive me,' asked Lola. 'There is no need to apologise, I shouldn't have interfered with your business. I didn't want you to get in too deep with the politics of the fashion house,' he replied. 'Mark, I know your heart was in the right place, I am sorry, let's forget it ever happen,' she said. 'Our first fight, the best part is making up,' Lola smiled, she knew what that meant. Mark told her he wants to check up on his mother and then he will come over to hers later tonight. Lola said she will be expecting him. Lola was so glad Mark called, she felt so bad she had made Mark so angry and the fact that; he was ready to make the first move that made her like him even more. Lola put off talking to Mark about genotype testing, things were already awkward; she didn't want to make things any worse. Lola went to make some Jollof rice for Mark; it was his favourite meal; she put the chicken in the oven and put a bottle of wine in the fridge, then she had a shower and put on her sexy nightgown, she was planning to make it up to Mark. Lola was sitting in front of the television when the doorbell went, 'oh my God, Mark must have driven over a hundred and ten miles per hour to get back here so quick, she thought out loud. Lola opened the door without asking who it was, Stefan marched in, 'who the hell do you think you are? How dare you go changing things around without asking my permission first? You women believe you can walk all over me whenever you feel like it.' Stefan was shouting and not allowing her to answer any of the questions he was throwing at her. 'First my ex-wife, then Bisi and now you. I won't tolerate any of your bullshit. I give you an inch you take a mile,' he then cursed at her in Italian, Stefan was intimidating, she has not seen him like this before, his eyes were bloodshot, and he was unshaven, he looked like the devil himself. Lola wanted to shout back at him, but she remained calm. 'I am sorry Stefan; I tried to call you, but you wouldn't return my calls,' she said. Stefan was now staring at Lola in her see-through night dress. Lola was trying to tell him that Bisi has been ripping off the fashion house for ages. Stefan was not listening; he was too busy admiring her; he could see her nipples through her nightdress. Stefan grabbed Lola towards him and kissed her on the lips, she felt butterflies in her stomach, only Stefan made her feel that way, she was just about to throw her arms around him, then Stefan pulled her away from him and said he was so sorry, he asked her to please forgive him and he ran out of the door. Lola just stood in the doorway stunned, ‘why do I let this man treat me this way?' She was so angry with herself, she knew she had to end it with Mark, she couldn’t have a loving relationship with Mark knowing she had feelings for Stefan.

Lola sat on the settee, going over what just happened, the doorbell went again; she went to answer the door it was Mark. Lola’s whole mood had changed. Mark thought it was because of the argument, they had earlier today. So, he did his best to make her feel better. They sat down and had dinner and watched a movie together, then they went to bed and made love. They talked about their day in Switzerland, Mark wanted to make love to her again, and then Lola just asked out of the blue. 'How would you feel taking a genotype test?' Asked Lola. Mark stopped caressing her breast. 'What is a genotype test?' Asked Mark. 'It’s a test you take to find out if you have inherited the sickle cell gene,' replied Lola. 'What is a sickle cell gene?' he asked. It surprised Lola that he didn’t know what a sickle cell gene is. 'Are you telling me you don’t know what sickle cell anaemia is?' Asked Lola. 'No, I don’t but, I am sure you will tell me all about it,' replied Mark. Mark lay on his back to listen to her explanation, he was thinking, what a killjoy she is. Sickle cell anaemia is an inherited blood disorder where the red blood cells, which carry oxygen around the body, develop abnormally. When the blood cells get stuck, it can cause tremendous pain. Lola told Mark that she is a sickle cell carrier and can pass the blood disorder on to her children if she has a child with another carrier. Lola also told Mark that, her first child died of sickle cell anaemia. Mark sat up when he realised the severity of what Lola was telling him. Mark then asked, are you saying that there’s a possibility that our children will only get the blood disorder if both of us are carriers of the sickle cell gene? 'Yes,' replied Lola. Mark told Lola that he has a daughter; she doesn’t have sickle cell; I don’t have the gene either. Lola asked him how he knew he didn't have the sickle cell gene and asked if he has taken the test? Mark said I don’t need to because I don’t have it. Lola was getting angry. 'Mark, we need to talk about this,' she said. 'No, we don’t, Anyway, why are we talking about having children, we are still getting to know each other? I don’t understand why you have brought this up now?

Are you pregnant?' Asked Mark. 'Don't be stupid,' she replied. 'Why is it a stupid question? Am I not good enough for you to have my child?' Asked Mark. 'If you have the sickle cell gene, I can't have children with you, that is the point I am trying to make,' replied Lola. 'I don't have a disease, so you need not worry, all this arguing is turning me on, let's make love again?' he said. Lola turned away from him; Mark was trying to dismiss what she had to say, and that made her annoyed. He caressed her breast again, Lola slapped his hand. He got on top of her and kissed her; Lola could feel his hardness against her leg. 'Mark then whispered to her; you are such a tease. 'He then slipped his hands between her legs, she was wet. 'You know you want me; ' he said. She then spread her legs giving him full access. Mark worked his magic on her, they both climaxed. Lola pushed him off her. Mark was lying on his back; he pulled Lola towards him and then fell asleep. Lola lay in his arms, she was, so contempt being there, she had even forgotten about Stefan's visit earlier. Lola would have to speak to Mark about taking the genotype test another day.

Chapter Eight

Stefan arrived home; he was so disgusted with himself, he couldn't believe he had forced himself on Lola, if he didn't stop himself, he would have taken advantage of her. The thought of that made him sick; he couldn't resist her and Lola made him so angry, but, he was falling in love with her; he didn't care about Bisi and her contract. In fact, he was glad that Lola had got rid of her. Bisi called him to say Lola had cancelled her order, and she was no longer the supplier of the fashion house. Stefan had a brief fling with Bisi, he tried to break it off with her, but Bisi threatened to tell his wife. The fact he cheated on his wife was eating Stefan up inside so, he spent most of the time at work, so he didn't have to face his wife. He hated lying to her; he loved his wife so much. Bisi used to work in the fashion house factory; Stefan and Bisi travelled together to meet with the fabric manufacturers. It was during their many trips to Switzerland; the affair started. Stefan had no choice but to send Bisi to the manufacturers on her own, just so he was not alone with her anymore. After six months, Bisi left the fashion house and opened her own shop in Liverpool street. Bisi demanded a five-year contract to supply to the fashion house. Stefan only agreed to a two-year contract and a verbal promise he will extend the contract for another three years if she maintained supplying high-quality material for the fashion house. Stefan knew the contract had expired, and he had no intention of extending it, he knew Lola didn't like her, and that Lola could run that side of the business herself. Stefan called off the affair with Bisi when his wife ran off with a younger man. Bisi had nothing to threaten him with anymore, he had ignored Lola's phone calls; his ego wouldn't allow him to call her back. Bisi's calling him to tell him, Lola had ended her contract, gave Stefan the perfect excuse to go to Lola's apartment.

Stefan took out a bottle of Italian wine from his wine cabinet and drowned his sorrows, he got so drunk, he couldn't move. Stefan could hear his phone ringing upstairs. He crawled upstairs, when he checked his phone, he could see a missed call from Bisi. 'What does this bitch want from me?' He cursed her in Italian, he then remembered that he had forgotten his bottle of wine downstairs. Stefan headed back downstairs, halfway down the stairs, he missed his footing and fell; hitting his head on the bannister, he fell head first at the bottom of the stairs. Stefan passed out; the cleaner found him the following morning and called the ambulance.

Lola's alarm woke her up, she went to the bathroom and brushed her teeth, she then got into the shower. When she came back into the bedroom, Mark was on top of the bed with his manhood erected. Good Morning, he said with a smile. Lola smiled at him and asked him to get ready for work. 'I will when you have said Good Morning properly,' he replied. Lola said she had just had a shower, he stood up and pulled her towards him. 'Have you got a water shortage?' Asked Mark. 'What do you mean?' Replied Lola. 'I mean, you can have another shower, we can have one together.' He put her on the bed and sucked on her breast; he knew it turned her on; she stopped resisting him; he lifted her leg up and slipped himself inside her. Mark, she groaned, he re-drew, he was teasing her, Lola took his penis and put it back inside her, he made love to her and they both climaxed. 'Wouldn't it be nice if we could stay here all day?' Asked Mark. 'Yes, it would be nice, but we both have work to do,' replied Lola. They both got in the shower together, after her second shower, she got out and got dressed; Mark was still in the bathroom brushing his teeth. They both had breakfast, and then they left for work. Mark dropped Lola off at the fashion house. 'When am I going to see you again?' Asked Mark. 'I will call you later.' replied Lola. She gave him a passionate kiss on the lips and walked into the fashion house. Lola was in her office; her voice mail was flashing, Lola called her mother and her designer in Lagos, she had a long conversation with her mother; she told her about Mark. Lola's mother insisted that Mark must take the genotype test and she must put a stop to the relationship until he has taken the test. Lola's mother knew her daughter has feelings for Stefan; she told her daughter that, she would be better off dating Stefan. Lola never told her mother how Stefan treated her, but Lola's mother could tell that she liked Stefan, whenever she mentioned Stefan's name it was always with adoration. Lola then spoke to her son; he had refused to go to school today because she didn't call him this morning, Temi thought something had happened to her. Lola reassured her son she was okay, 'Temi, you must never refuse to go to school,' she said. There will be days when I will be busy, and I won't be able to call you in the morning. I will always make sure I speak to you before you go to bed. Lola felt guilty, the only reason she didn’t call Temi this morning, was because she was with Mark. She asked Temi to promise not to refuse to go to school again. 'I promise mummy; ' he said. 'What are you going to do for the rest of the day?' Asked Lola. 'I will help grandma this morning; the lesson teacher is coming in the afternoon,' replied Temi. Temi told his mother about the new PE teacher that started at his school; Lola listened for a while and then she told him to give the phone to his grandma. 'My daughter make sure you speak to Mark about going to do his genotype test,' she said. 'I will mother; I will call you later;’ said Lola. She didn’t want her mother to continue nagging her. Lola then called the designer to find out if her Lace had arrived, he confirmed it had. 'I will text you my measurement later,' said Lola. 'Madam, are you coming to Lagos for the wedding too?' Asked the designer. 'Yes, I am, the Minister’s wife invited me,' replied Lola. 'That’s good, we look forward to your visit,' he said. 'Thank you, I will speak to you tomorrow.' 'Goodbye,' she said. 'Goodbye madam,' he replied. Stefan personal assistant came into Lola’s office, 'have you heard?' 'Heard what?' Asked Lola. 'Stefan is in the hospital in a coma,' she said. 'What happened?' Lola shouted. The personal assistant told Lola that Stefan fell down the stairs and hit his head; he broke his left arm. He had been drinking she said, the level of alcohol in his bloodstream was high, something must have upset him; he only drinks when he is angry, said the personal assistant. Lola felt guilty; he had left her house last night, and he was furious. 'When did this happen?' Asked Lola. 'It happened last night, but the cleaner only found him this morning,' replied the personal assistant. 'Oh no, so he was alone all night, I must go to the hospital,' said Lola. 'What's the name of the hospital?' Asked Lola. Stefan's personal assistant told her he was at the Chelsea and Westminster Hospital. Lola grabbed her bag and told the personal assistant she needs to see Stefan. When she got to the reception desk, she asked the receptionist to call a taxi. Stefan's personal assistant came running after her from the office, remember he is in a coma, so calm down. Lola was not listening, she waved down the taxi as he was driving up to the fashion house. 'Where do you want to go?' Asked the taxi man. 'I am going to the Chelsea and Westminster Hospital,' replied Lola.

Lola went to the reception desk to find out which ward Stefan was in, she had forgotten to ask Stefan's personal assistant, what the name of the ward was. The receptionist directed her to the ward on the fourth floor, Lola arrived at admissions; the nurse asked if she was a relative; she told the nurse she is Stefan's girlfriend. The nurse looked surprised by that; she walked her to his private room; he was still in a coma and breathing aided by a ventilator. The nurse told her not to worry, that he looked worse than he is, Lola stood over him and kissed him on the forehead. 'I am so sorry Stefan; I didn't mean to upset you.' She held his right hand and promised not to leave his side. Lola told Stefan about her trip to Switzerland and how he will love the Lace material she bought for the fashion house. Stefan's brother Gianni walked into the room. 'How is he doing?' he asked.' Apart from his broken arm, he is stable,' replied Lola. 'Haven't I seen you before?' Asked Lola. 'Yes, you have, Stefan brought you to my restaurant in Soho, I am his older brother,' replied Gianni. 'Yes, I remember now, a very nice restaurant and the food was delicious,' Lola said. 'Thank you,' said Gianni. 'my brother likes you; he is always talking about you,' said Gianni. 'I am surprised about that; your brother is such a pain in the backside,' replied Lola. Gianni smiled at her. 'I know he is, his own worst enemy,' said Gianni. They both laughed out loud. Gianni stayed for two hours; they talked and took turns in reading the Daily Times to Stefan, he always reads the Daily Times. Gianni had to leave to open his restaurant, and he wanted to know if Lola needed a lift home. Lola said she can't leave Stefan, and that she wants to be here when he wakes up. Gianni said he will come back as soon as his staff arrive, he also said he would bring Lola something nice to eat. 'Thank you, Gianni. That's kind of you.'

Lola sat on Stefan's bed and told him how much she loved him; she apologised for causing him so much pain, I hope when you wake up you can do the same. Lola swore she saw his hand move, I know you can hear me, as per usual, you are ignoring me. If you ask me to marry you, the answer will be yes. You can take me to Italy; I heard it's such a lovely place. Stefan personal assistant came into the room. 'Hello Lola, has there been any change?' She asked. 'Not yet, although I saw his hand move as I was speaking to him,' said Lola. The personal assistant said, even though people are in a coma, they can still, hear what people are saying to them. 'Are you serious?' Asked Lola. Lola was hoping he was not listening to her telling him she would marry him, she felt embarrassed; the nurse came in to check him over. The personal assistant went to buy cups of tea, the nurse asked Lola if she will spend the night. Lola didn’t think of that, but she had no intention of leaving Stefan alone. 'Yes, I am,' she said. The nurse said she would make up a bed for her. 'Thank you very much,' replied Lola. The personal assistant came back with the tea. I have a few things for you to sign on behalf of Stefan, it’s very urgent. She gave the paperwork to Lola, I will pick them up in the morning. Lola promised to read them tonight and sign them ready for her in the morning. Stefan’s personal assistant sat with her and Stefan for another half an hour then left. Lola took the paperwork out of the folder and read the documents to Stefan. Since you can hear me, I will read the documents and sign them on your behalf, you can’t then accuse me of trying to run your life for you, she smiled as she said that. At eight o’clock, Gianni walked into the room with a takeaway dish. 'Hello Lola, what are you doing?' He Asked. 'Hello Gianni, I am reading these documents to Stefan, so; he knows what I am doing on his behalf,' replied Lola. Gianni smiled. 'You are such a lovely girl, now I know why Stefan likes you.' He gave her the food he had brought with him. It was a lovely spaghetti Bolognese, with lots of cheese on top, it was so delicious. The nurse came in to make up the bed for Lola. 'Are you spending the night?' Gianni asked. 'Yes, I wouldn't be able to sleep at home, knowing he was here alone, I need to pop back and get an overnight bag, can you please stay and wait for me to get back?' Gianni asked if she wanted him to give her a lift home, Lola said no she will take a taxi, I don't want Stefan left alone. Gianni said he would wait until she gets back. Lola told him she will be as quick as possible, Gianni told her to take her time. Lola left the hospital and turned her phone back on, she had several messages from Mark, her mother had called too, she called her mother back; she knew it would be Temi wondering why she had not called him. Hello mother, how are you? 'I am fine, Temi wanted to speak to you', replied her mother. 'Is he still awake?' 'Yes, he is, he refused to sleep; he said he is waiting for his mother to call him'. Lola asked to speak to Temi so he can go to bed. Temi told his mother about his day and how he got the maths questions the lesson teacher gave him all right. Lola told him how proud she was of him, she told him to keep up the good work and that she will buy him a nice present when she comes over for Christmas. 'Go to bed now and think about the present you want me to buy for you for Christmas,' she said. 'Okay mummy, Goodnight,' he said. 'Goodnight my darling,' she replied. Temi gave the phone to his grandmother. 'My daughter, have you had a hectic day?' Asked Lola's mother. 'No, Stefan fell down the stairs last night; he is in the hospital in a coma,' she replied. 'Oh no, is he going to be okay? Asked Lola's mother. 'The doctors said we won't know how serious his injuries are until he wakes up. I am hoping there's no brain damage,' replied Lola. 'Brain damage, that sounds serious?' Asked Lola's mother. 'I know it sounds serious, but I am praying for him,' said Lola. Lola's mother said she will pray for him too. 'I must go now mother, I need to go back to the hospital, I will speak to you tomorrow.' 'Okay, my daughter, don't worry too much God is in control,' she said. 'Amen,' replied Lola. Lola wasn't a churchgoer, but she believed in God, she had been praying all day for Stefan to make a full recovery. Lola returned Mark's call. 'Hello stranger, where have you been all day?' Asked Mark. 'I have been at the hospital, Stefan had a fall; he is in a coma,' replied Lola. 'Why is your phone switched off?' Asked Mark. 'I have been in the hospital; ' she replied. 'That does not mean you can't have your phone on, Mark responded. 'Why are you questioning me like this? Don't you care about

Stefan being in a coma?' Asked Lola. 'Why should I care about Stefan? He is taking up too much of my girlfriend's time,' replied Mark. 'I can't speak to you when you are being like this, I will call you tomorrow,' she said. 'Why tomorrow? I am coming over now,' he replied. 'No, you can't I am on my way back to the hospital,' replied Lola. 'If you are not at your apartment when I get there, don't call me again,' said Mark. 'Don't waste your time driving to my apartment; I am on the way back to the hospital,' replied Lola. The phone went dead. Lola was so appalled by Mark's behaviour, but she didn't have time to think about his jealousy tonight. Stefan was her priority. Lola arrived at the hospital it was eleven o'clock. Gianni was reading the Daily Times to his brother. 'How is he?' Lola asked. 'No change yet, I am leaving now, so I can get to the restaurant before it closes at midnight, do you need anything before I leave?' Asked Gianni. 'No thank you, I have everything I need right here,' replied Lola. 'Please call me if there are any changes, it doesn't matter what time it is, I will check on you both tomorrow morning unless you call me,' said Gianni. 'Lola, what is your number?' Asked Gianni. Lola read out her number; he typed it into his phone, he rang her and told her to save his name and number in her phone contacts. Gianni kissed Lola on both cheeks and said see you tomorrow. Lola smiled back and said, “thank you for the food”. Goodnight Gianni. Gianni had set up the bed, he is such a kind and thoughtful guy. Lola continued to read the document’s that Stefan’s personal assistant brought for her to sign. When she finished reading them, she told Stefan, she was about to sign the documents and she asked Stefan if it was okay with him? Stefan moved his right eyebrow, Lola shouted for the nurse with excitement, the nurse came running in, 'whatever is the matter?' Asked the nurse. 'Stefan moved his right eyebrow, that’s a good sign isn't it?' Asked Lola. 'Yes, that is a good sign,' replied the nurse. The nurse checked the machine to see if there was brain movement recorded, there was. The nurse told Lola not to worry that the doctor will see Stefan in the morning. Lola said a prayer for Stefan and fell asleep as soon as her head hit the pillow, she was so tired.

The sound of the alarm woke Lola up, the alarm goes off at six o’clock every day, she sat up to look over at Stefan, he was lying on his right side looking at her. Lola jumped out of the bed and went over to Stefan; he was smiling at her.

'Stefan, are you okay? How long have you been awake? Are you in pain?' Asked Lola. 'How many God damn questions do you want me to answer at once?' Replied Stefan. 'I can see you are back to your grumpy old self, let me call the nurse to put you back to sleep,' said Lola. Stefan tried to laugh, but he couldn't. Lola pressed the button for the nurse. 'Stay still; I have been so worried about you,' she said. 'Answer me one thing, Lola,' said Stefan. 'What do you want to know?' Asked Lola. 'Did you spend the night here with me?' he asked. 'Isn't it obvious I did? Do you think I would leave you alone like this?' Asked Lola. The nurse came in just as he was about to answer. 'How long have you been awake Mr Gotie?' Asked the nurse. 'Not long, her snoring woke me up,' he replied. They both looked at Lola and laughed. 'Can you give him something to put him back to sleep? I think I preferred him when he was quiet,' replied Lola. The nurse smiled and checked all his vital stats, she helped Stefan sit up and told him she would call the doctor, she left the room. Stefan pulled Lola closer to him. 'Do you want me to go back to sleep?' Asked Stefan. 'No, don't you ever put me through that again,' she replied. 'Put you through what? You don't even like me,' replied Stefan. 'I like you; in fact, I am in love with you,'

Lola said. Stefan looked surprised, 'so why have you been having it off with that wimp?' Asked Stefan. 'What do you mean having it off with that wimp?' replied Lola. ‘I know you have been shagging that Mark, haven't you?’ Asked Stefan. Lola was so embarrassed; she didn’t want to admit to Stefan that she was having sex with Mark. 'Answer me, woman? You know how to drive a man crazy,' he said. 'If you were trying to make me jealous, you have succeeded,' said Stefan. 'Stefan, you need to calm down, you have only just come out of a coma,' said Lola. 'Yes, the one you put me in,' replied Stefan. Lola couldn’t believe she was having a row with Stefan over Mark. Lola was fighting the tears back; she blamed herself for Stefan being in the hospital. 'Haven’t you got anything to say for yourself?' Asked Stefan. 'Why are you being like this?' Asked Lola? 'Like what?' Asked Stefan. Lola shouted at Stefan; 'my love life is none of your business.' 'Oh, so you are not even denying it?' Asked Stefan. 'I have just come back from a near-death experience, all you want to do is argue with me,' he said. 'You started it,' replied Lola. You're the one that has been shagging Mark, and you expect me to be okay with it,' replied Stefan. 'I am not arguing with you anymore; I am getting ready for work, damn you,

Stefan,' she said as she headed for the door. 'I tried to be nice to you, and you threw it back in my face,' she said. Stefan's face was turning red, Lola knew when he gets like that, his whole demeanour changes. 'I think you need to calm down,' she said. 'Who is paying you to think?' Stefan shouted he jerked his left hand he screamed in pain. Lola rushed over to him. 'Look what you made me do,' he said. 'Stefan, you are nothing but a miserable git. ' Lola plucked the pillow to make him comfortable, as she did that, Stefan pulled her toward him with his right hand. 'The only miserable git here is you, but I wouldn't love you any other way,' he replied. He kissed her, Lola kissed him back, she felt the butterflies in her stomach again, she had missed him so much, Lola pulled away and told him she loved him. 'I love you too,' Stefan replied, she was just about to kiss him again, then the doctor and the nurse walked him.

Hello Stefan, glad to have you back in the land of the living, you gave us all a scare, said the doctor. The doctor and Stefan are old acquaintances, I will book you in for a scan tomorrow if everything comes back okay, you can go home. 'Your arm will stay in the plaster for six weeks. How are you feeling? Do you have a headache?' Asked the doctor. 'Apart from the one standing over there, I am fine,' replied Stefan. Lola was rolling her eyes at him. Stefan told the doctor he needed a rest from Lola, the doctor told him that next time he fancies a rest, not to throw himself down the stairs, he should go on holiday instead. The doctor and Stefan both laughed out loud. 'I walked into that one, didn't I?' Asked Stefan. 'Yes, you did Stefan,' replied the doctor. The doctor told him he will see him tomorrow morning at eleven o'clock. Stefan and Lola thanked the doctor and the nurse, then they both left the room. 'Where were we?' Asked Stefan. Lola said he was just telling her how much he loved her. 'I might have banged my head, but, it was you telling me how much you loved me,' said Stefan. 'I will not argue with you,' said Lola. 'Go ahead, argue with me, I like a good argument, you speak so eloquently, replied Stefan. 'What do you mean I speak so eloquently?' Asked Lola. 'You don't speak like most black women,' replied Stefan. Lola was gobsmacked, 'what are you trying to say? You sound racist,' shouted Lola. 'How does saying you speak eloquently make me a racist? What are you talking about Lola? I am offended,' replied Stefan. 'I am also offended that, you said I don't speak like most black women, it's all

coming out now, I wondered how long it would take before the white supremacy lines came out,' shouted Lola. 'Just get ready for work Lola, I don't understand how we got here, this argument is absurd,' said Stefan. 'Let me educate you then, white supremacist always justifies their supremacy by saying stupid things to black people like you talk eloquently, you have good hair or skin, and the most popular one is, how can I be racist, I have black friends? Its subliminal racism because they are hoping their racist remarks will go unnoticed by those they wish to offend. 'Stefan, you said I speak eloquently and not like most black women, you are almost saying I am equal to you but, other black women are not,' said Lola. 'Lola, this discussion is getting too technical for me, it wasn't a racist comment, I was
being complimentary,' said Stefan. 'Telling me I speak eloquently was complimentary, but, your justification for saying so, was racist,' replied Lola. 'I see your point now, I will have to watch what I say to you from now on,' Stefan said. 'No Stefan, you don't have to watch what you say because, if you are not a white supremacist you won't have to worry about what you say, it might just be subconscious, and I will be here to call you out every time,' replied Lola. 'All this talk

about racism has turned me on, I want to rip your clothes off, but, I only have the use of one of my hand,' said Stefan. 'Lola smiled, you can do that another day,' replied Lola. 'I want you here and now,' said Stefan. Stefan took Lola's hand and put it under the covers, so she could feel his hardness. Lola said there is no way she is making love to him in a hospital bed, she told him he needed a shower to cool off. Lola called the nurse, to find out if Stefan could have a shower, the nurse said he could have a shower so she helped Stefan to get undressed and led him to the bathroom, they both brushed their teeth and Lola put on the shower for him. 'Lola, I need help with scrubbing my back.' shouted Stefan. 'Lola came to help him; he pulled her in, she was still wearing her nightie. Stefan kissed her; she was soaking wet, she was as good as naked, that drove him wild, he was struggling to take her nightie off, Lola helped him, that gave him the green light, he knew she wanted him as much as he wanted her. Stefan pinned her to the wall so he could use his right hand at ease, he sucked on her breast, she was groaning, he then sat on the disabled chair Lola sat on his laps', they kissed and then he was inside her, Lola was riding him as if her life depended on it. They both climaxed. Stefan made her promise never to leave him.

'Stefan, I will never leave you. I love you,' she said. They finished their shower and Lola called Gianni to let him know Stefan was awake.

Gianni arrived, to see his little brother sitting up and responsive, he kissed Stefan on both cheeks. 'What's wrong with you? Don't you ever do that to us again? You had us both worried sick,' said Gianni. 'I am sorry big brother; I promise to be more careful next time,' replied Stefan. 'Well, I know Lola will take proper care of you now,' said Gianni. 'I will leave you to talk,' said Lola. 'Where are you going?' Asked Stefan. 'I am going home to change, and I need to go to the fashion house, some of us need to work and I am expecting a delivery from Switzerland today,' replied Lola. 'Gianni, she tried to kill me so she could take over my business,' said Stefan. 'No, I didn't, you were drunk and fell down the stairs,' she said. 'Why was I drunk? Asked Stefan. Because you are a silly man that can't handle his drink,' she replied. 'No Lola, it's because you were driving me crazy,' replied Stefan. 'I am not listening to this; I will leave you with your brother and maybe he can talk sense into you,' said Lola. 'Lola, I can't help you there. I have been trying to talk sense into my brother for years, he doesn't listen,' replied Gianni. 'I can imagine, he is a stubborn mule,' Lola replied. 'It takes one to know one,' shouted Stefan. Lola went over to Stefan and kissed him; 'I will be back soon,' she said. 'Hurry back; I don't want my brother to bore me to tears,' he replied. Lola went over to Gianni and kissed him on the cheeks, 'I am sorry I have to leave you with this pain in the backside, but someone has to put up with him,' said Lola. Gianni laughed at her joke. Gianni then said, 'if he gives me any trouble I will knock him out again'. Lola smiled and left the room.

Lola got home; she lay on her bed thinking about Stefan, she didn't realise how much she loved him. Lola called her mother; she needed to talk to someone, her mother was the only person she could talk to about her feeling. 'Hello, mother,' Lola said. 'Hello, my daughter, how are you? Are you at work?' She asked. 'No, I am at home; I have just returned home from the hospital,' said Lola. 'Okay, how is Mark?' Asked Lola's mother. 'Not, Mark, it's Stefan, Lola was quick to correct her. 'Sorry, my mistake, how is Stefan?' 'He is fine; he woke up in the early hours of this morning, apart from his arm, he is well,' she smiled to herself. 'You sound thrilled, have you had your wicked way with him?' Asked

Lola's Mother. 'Mother!' She shouted. My daughter, I know you well. 'I know there must be a good reason you are calling me at this time of the day, you must need my advice. 'Anyway, I was waiting for you to call me,' she said. 'What is the matter, mother?' Lola Asked. 'Alhaji came to see me yesterday; he is not happy with the fact, he has not heard from you in over a month,' said Lola's mother. 'I hope you explained to him I have been busy?' Asked Lola. 'I did, and he understands, he is coming to London next week on a business trip. Lola said she will call him, she is looking forward to seeing him again, she has missed him so much. 'Is that what you wanted to tell me, mother?' Asked Lola. 'No, my daughter, Alhaji and I were talking about Mark; I told him you and Mark are getting close, but you want him to do a genotype test but, he is refusing to do one. Alhaji is insisting he does the test because Mark's father died of complications of sickle cell anaemia,' said Lola's mother. 'Oh, my God,' Lola shouted. 'Mark told me he didn't know what sickle cell anaemia was, said Lola. 'Well, he might not know what it is; he never knew his father. Mark believed his father died after a bout of malaria. That was half of the truth, Mark's father had malaria that brought on the sickle cell complications.' Lola looked confused,

'I thought they said, if you have sickle cell anaemia, you are immune from malaria?' Asked Lola. 'That is not true, people with sickle cell disease can get malaria, but the malaria symptoms are not as bad. Anyway, the bottom line is that Mark needs to do the genotype test, his refusing to do one is alarming. When did you speak to him last?' Asked Lola's mother. 'I spoke to him yesterday, but he told me not to call him again,' replied Lola. 'Why?' Asked Lola's mother. 'He didn't want me to see Stefan in the hospital, he made me chose between him and Stefan,' replied Lola. 'Oh, bless him, you have two good men fighting over you, who are you going to choose?' Asked Lola's mother. 'I love Stefan, I wouldn't have lead Mark on if Stefan wasn't playing nasty games with me,' said Lola. 'Why did Stefan treat you like that? That was very childish of him,' said Lola's mother. 'I know, he is so insecure, his brother told me that, he changed after his wife ran off with a younger man so, he trusts no one. One minute he is okay, the next minute he is a manic depressive, he even tried to kill himself because he blames himself for his failed marriage.' 'Oh, my God, are you sure you can handle such a man? If he has all these trust issues, it might affect your relationship with him, said Lola's mother. 'I can handle him, he needs the love of a good woman, replied Lola. 'Please talk to him about his insecurities,' replied Lola's mother. 'I will, as soon as he gets home, I will take him on holiday; he needs a break,' said Lola. 'What are you going to do about Mark?' Asked Lola's mother. 'I don't know yet. I will wait for Alhaji to come next week,' replied Lola. 'Why are you waiting for Alhaji to come next week? I can tell already that you have chosen Stefan over Mark,' said Lola's mother. 'What do you mean mother?' Asked Lola. 'You can't use the excuse that Mark might have the sickle cell trait as the reason for your break up. Mark deserves to know the truth; I suspect he already knows,' said Lola's mother. 'Mark won't take my calls, he won't listen to anything I have to say,' replied Lola. 'Lola, make him listen and do it sooner rather than later,' said Lola's mother. 'Okay, mother, I will call him,' replied Lola. 'Lola, promise me you will call Mark?' Asked Lola's mother. 'I promise,' replied Lola. 'How is Temi?' Asked Lola. He is fine, he asked about you this morning, I told him, you will call when he gets back from school, said Lola's mother. 'Okay, I will call you later. Bye, mother.' 'Goodbye, my daughter.'

Lola was so sleepy; she went to sleep for two hours, talking about Mark and Stefan was exhausting. Lola felt so ashamed for leading Mark on; she had promised herself when she left Nigeria that, she would never have a relationship with a black man without knowing their genotype. The big question is when is the best time to talk to your partner about a genotype test? Is it a question you ask at the start of a relationship or just before you get married? What kind of loving relationship can you be in if you can switch your love off for someone just because they have sickle cell anaemia or the trait? Lola was so glad she had a chat with her mother. One thing about her mother, she would always tell you the truth, no matter how painful it was.

Lola called the fashion house; the delivery had already arrived, she told the Office Manager she would be in at two in the afternoon. She set the alarm for one o’clock, and she went to sleep. The alarm went off; Lola got up and got herself ready to go to the office. She called Stefan; he was not happy that she was taking so long. 'What time are you coming back here? He asked. 'I am not sure; I am on my way to the office now,' she replied. 'What have you been doing all morning?

Asked Stefan. I spoke to my mother, slept for two hours, that hospital bed is so uncomfortable, she said. 'I am tired, bored and there is nothing but rubbish on the television, no one cares about me,' he said. 'Self-pity doesn't suit you,' replied Lola. 'That's rich coming from you,' said Stefan. 'Stefan, what are you talking about now?' Asked Lola. 'Nothing Lola, get here whenever it is convenient for you,' he replied. 'Stefan, I am not talking to you while you are like this, said Lola. 'Like what?' He shouted down the phone. 'Needy,' she shouted back. 'Who are you calling needy? I am still your leader,' said Stefan. 'Stefan, stop your noise, you couldn't lead yourself out of a paper bag so please leave the leading to the expert's,' Lola replied. 'I suppose you are the so-called expert,' he asked? 'You got that right, I will be there soon,' replied Lola. 'Did Stacey come and collect the documents I signed?' Asked Lola. 'Yes, she did, there you go signing my life away again, he said. 'Stefan, get a grip, you might be a great lover, but, you are a rubbish patient,' said Lola. Stefan laughed at that comment. 'Okay, Lola, I am sitting here waiting for you, that's if I don't die of boredom first, said Stefan. 'My darling, I will be there as soon as I can,' she said. 'Make it sooner rather than later; I am getting turned on just talking to you,' he said. Lola was blushing. 'Stefan, you are such a sex maniac, she said. Lola, that’s what you have turned me into,' he replied. 'I will speak to you later, said Lola. Stefan called her name again, just as she was about to put the phone down. 'What do you want now?' she asked. 'I wanted to say how much I love you,’ said Stefan. ‘I love you too Stefan,’ replied Lola. Lola arrived at the fashion house at a quarter past two, she went to see the Office Manager and the designer from Kenya; they were both impressed with the Lace she ordered. The designer said the outfits would be ready for the Milan fashion show in two weeks’ time. They talked about the models they would use for the Milan show. They all agreed that they would use models from London. The designer told Lola that Mr Goite prefers Italian models, Lola said this time we will use English models because Mr Goite will not be attending the fashion show. Since he is the only one who speaks Italian, it would be very difficult for us to communicate what we want. They agreed a time and a date for the viewing, the meeting had gone on for two hours. When she got to her office, it was four thirty, she had to type out a five-year contract for her manufacturer in Switzerland, she had given him the contract to supply to the fashion house for the next five years. The fashion house was the only UK based establishment that designed clothes for high street stores, the fashion house didn’t use sweatshops, they had an in-house factory, and they used the best designers from all over the world. Lola was one of such designers. Stefan had headhunted both Lola and the designer from Kenya, to cover the African side of the business. African fabric has become popular in the Western part of the world. A lot of women are now wearing Kaftans made from African fabrics. It has become so popular, during the summer periods. Her phone rang, and Stefan’s name flashed up on her phone. 'Hello Stefan, how are you?' Asked Lola. 'I am bored when are you coming? It’s six o’clock, said Stefan. 'Stefan, I am so sorry, my meeting with Steve and David went on for longer than expected. I have just finished drafting a contract for the supplier in Switzerland. Have you read and signed the documents, I left with you this morning?' asked Lola. 'Yes, I have, I was so bored, I have read the contract five times already,' replied Stefan. 'Okay, I am on my way, I will see you soon. Do you want anything?' Asked Lola. 'Yes, I want you here by my side now,' he replied. 'I meant if you wanted something to eat?' Asked Lola. 'No, my brother has just left, and he brought us some food, I am so hungry, but, I am not eating until you get here, replied Stefan. 'Okay my darling, I will be there in thirty minutes,' she replied. 'I am waiting,' he said. Lola told him he doesn't have a choice but to wait for her, she disconnected the phone because she knew he would say something sarcastic in return.

Lola arrived at the hospital with her overnight bag forty-five minutes later, she had to go back to the fashion house halfway on route to the hospital, she had forgotten the overnight bag in the office. Stefan was too tired to argue with Lola when she arrived at the hospital, she gave him a passionate kiss on the lips, has she wanted to move away, he pulled her onto the bed. He found it difficult to resist Lola. 'Oh, my God, I have missed you so much,' he said. 'I missed you too Stefan, but one of us needs to keep us in a job,' she replied. 'He laughed, I thought women can do several things at the same time?' Asked Stefan. 'What do you mean?' Asked Lola. 'You can keep us in a job and attend to my every need,' he replied. 'Well, I am here now, what do you want me to do for you?' Asked Lola. Stefan lifted the sheets up to show her his bulge. 'I can’t help you with that,' she said. 'Why not?' He asked. 'This is a hospital,' she replied. So, what?' he replied. 'You can lock the door, or we can go for another shower,' he replied. Lola was blushing again. 'Stop it, let's eat, I am hungry,' said Lola. Lola got off the bed and went to warm the food in the microwave, they both sat at the table and ate the food Gianni had bought for them.

'Lola, how was your day?' Asked Stefan. 'It was okay; I got everything done, in so little time, even with all your distractions,' she replied. Lola told Stefan about her meeting with Steve and David, Stefan isn't happy, Lola is using British models instead of Italian models. After Lola explained her reasons, Stefan agreed with her. 'Why can't I go to the Italian fashion show?' Asked Stefan. Lola told him he needs to rest, Stefan said if he rests anymore, he might as well be dead. She smacked his hand and told him not to joke about things like that. Lola told him he will have to wait and see what the doctor says tomorrow. 'After speaking to the doctor, I will decide if you can go or not,' said Lola. 'Yes, mummy,' he replied. 'I will ignore that,' she replied. They talked more about work. Stefan told her what he needed her to do at the office. Gianni called Stefan; they were both talking on the phone speaking Italian. Lola cleared the plates away. Stefan gave Lola the phone; my brother wants to talk to you. 'Hello Gianni, how are you?' Asked Lola. 'I am fine thank you,' he replied. 'How are you, Lola?' Asked Gianni. 'I am well,' she replied. 'Are you coming down after work,' she asked? 'No, not tonight, I will come in the morning, before Stefan goes for his scan,' said Gianni. 'Thanks for the food, it was delicious as usual,' said Lola. 'You are welcome, see you in the morning,' replied Gianni. 'Goodnight Gianni,' said Lola.

Stefan was trying to get undressed so he can have a shower, Lola went over to him to help him get undressed. He grabbed Lola and pulled her towards him; she could feel his hardness on her leg. 'The choice is yours,' he said. 'What are you talking about Stefan?' Asked Lola. 'You can either get into the shower dressed, or you can take your clothes off now,' he replied. She smiled at him and took off her blouse. Stefan unclips her bra, exposing her breast, he held her right breast in his hand, he bent down to suck on it. Lola took off her skirt and her panties. Stefan didn’t make it to the bathroom; he took her to the bed and made love to her. Stefan got of Lola and sat up on the bed. 'What’s the matter, my love,' she asked? You can never tell when Stefan's mood will change, she was sitting up next to him. He turned around and said to her, 'promise me you will never leave me?' He asked. 'I promise,' she responded. Stefan was feeling insecure again. Lola felt so sorry for him. Lola got up and directed him towards the bathroom, they both had a shower together. Lola was drying Stefan's back, and she said, she will miss this shower and that she loved having a shower with him. Stefan told her, his shower at his house is bigger than the whole of the hospital bathroom. Lola asked him if this was his way of asking her to move in with him? 'How are you going to care for me if you don't move in?' Asked Stefan. 'Do I need to move in with you to be your carer?' Asked Lola. 'My requirements need a live-in carer,' he replied. 'Don't worry honey; I will arrange an interview with a live-in carer,' said Lola. He turned around to face her; 'I don't just want anyone, I want you and If you behave, I might upgrade you to a live-in girlfriend', Stefan said. 'You are so generous. I will tend to your every need and I will be on my best behaviour,' replied Lola. 'Lola! On her best behaviour that will be a first,' replied Stefan. 'You will boss me around as soon as you get your feet under the table,' said Stefan. 'Someone needs to keep you in check,' she replied. Stefan put his boxers and T-shirt back on, while Lola put on her see-through night dress. 'You are such a tease,' said Stefan. Lola just rolled her eyes at him. They both climbed into the bed and watched a movie on the laptop. Halfway through the film, Lola fell asleep on Stefan's chest. She was in a foetus position; it must have been the sound of his heartbeat. The nurse came in to take Stefan temperature; Lola got up. 'Did you enjoy the movie,' he asked? Lola elbowed him. 'Did you enjoy it, Stefan?' Asked Lola. 'Yes, I did, the best thing about it, I didn't have to listen to any more of your running commentary for the rest of the film,' replied Stefan. The nurse looked at Lola and asked how does she put up with him? 'With much difficulty, but, he is loveable,' Lola replied. 'Lola, you are a joker,' he said. If I wasn't here, you would whine like a baby,' replied Lola. Lola made up the bed for her to sleep in. 'What are you doing?' Asked Stefan. 'I want to go to bed, I am so tired,' she said. 'Come and get back into bed with me,' he insisted. 'No, that bed is too small for the two of us,' she replied. 'You are just going to make do with it for tonight, tomorrow night you can enjoy my king-size bed, said Stefan. There was no point arguing with Stefan, it was best to just let him have his own way for peace of mind. Lola turned off the light and snuggled up to Stefan.

Lola's alarm went off at six in the morning, she tried to reach for it and almost fell out of the bed. 'Why did you set the alarm for six anyway?' Asked Stefan. 'I didn't that's the time I always get up,' replied Lola. Lola got out of the bed, 'where are you going now?' Asked Stefan. 'To brush my teeth,' she replied. 'Why don't you stay in bed? I am not seeing the doctor until eleven o'clock,' Stefan said. 'I am up now, so I might as well have a shower,' Lola replied. Stefan just ignored her. Lola finished brushing her teeth and got in the shower, she kind of half expected Stefan to join her, but he didn't, she got dressed and told Stefan that she is off to get some hot drinks, he made a noise as if he was acknowledging her. Lola ignored him too; she knew he was in one of his moods. By the time, she got back to the room, Stefan was in the shower. Lola sat down to enjoy her coffee and called her mother and spoke to Temi. Stefan was out of the shower now; he had a T-shirt and his boxers on. Stefan picked up his coffee and took a sip, he was trying to get Lola's attention, she was ignoring him. Stefan threw bits of paper at her. Lola covered the mouthpiece of the phone and told Stefan he was acting like a child. He pulled his tongue out at her, he would have said something nasty, but he knew she was on the phone with her son. Gianni walked in; he had brought them a lovely breakfast. The hospital food was nice, but Gianni never gave them the opportunity to eat the food at the hospital. He brought food in for them all day long. Stefan told his brother that Lola was ignoring him, 'lovers tiff, is it?' Asked Gianni. Lola hurried up to finish her phone call, she told Gianni that Stefan is a right little bully. The nurse and the porter came in to take Stefan for a brain scan.

The doctor came in with the results of the scan, it was all clear, the doctor told Stefan that he will discharge him today and he only had to come back to the outpatients for them to check on the progress on his broken arm. Lola packed Stefan things; Gianni would drive them to Stefan house. Stefan lived on Montpelier Square in Knightsbridge. Lola had never been to Stefan's house; she was so impressed when she saw his house. Stefan's house was occupying one of the best positions, south facing and overlooking the square garden, the elegant period townhouse arranged over six floors and with a lift. Stefan's house was breath-taking. The interior design was of the highest specifications incorporated. 'This house is beautiful,' Lola said. 'I am glad you like it,' Stefan replied. 'This house is too big for you alone to live-in,' said Lola. 'I have been telling him to sell this place for over three years, but he won't listen,' Gianni replied. 'Will you two stop trying to run my life for me, the house might be empty now, but when the children come over, and the family from Italy are here, there is nowhere to sling a cat,' Stefan said. Lola then noticed the elevator, 'oh my God; there is a lift in here too? How come you fell down the stairs?' Asked Lola. 'The man was drunk he didn't remember he had a lift,' Gianni replied. Lola laughed at Gianni's joke, Stefan just ignored them both and took the lift to the master bedroom. Gianni showed Lola the rest of the house when Stefan gets into a mood, he is best left alone. Gianni showed Lola the master bedroom, they went into the room, and Stefan was sitting on the bed staring into thin air. 'Are you okay?' Lola asked. 'I am okay; I am just tired, someone woke me up at six o'clock this morning,' replied Stefan. They left Stefan in the room, and Gianni continued to show her the rest of the house. Gianni left after showing Lola around the house; 'I need to get back to the restaurant, look after my brother for me. I know he is a pain, but you know how to handle him, said Gianni. 'I will do my best, if he drives me round the bend, I will throw him down the stairs again,' Gianni laughed and kissed her on both cheeks and left. Lola returned to the master bedroom, and Stefan was lying on the bed. He patted the bed gesturing her to join him. They both lay on the bed together, Lola snuggled up to Stefan and went to sleep, she woke up two hours later aroused because Stefan was sucking on her breast, they made love and fell asleep again.

Chapter Nine

Waking up the following morning in Stefan's bed felt strange, she wants to wake up next to Stefan for the rest of her life. Lola was up and getting ready for work, she was finding it very difficult to get Stefan up and ready. All he wanted to do was stay in bed with her. 'The doctor might have signed you off but, I must go to work,' said Lola. 'You don't have to do anything you don't want to do,' said Stefan. 'That's my point, Stefan, I want to go to work,' replied Lola. 'Have you had enough of me already?' Asked Stefan. 'I will never have enough of you but, I don't want to be a kept woman,' replied Lola. The doctor advised Stefan not to go to work for at least four weeks; he needed to rest. Stefan was not willing to sit at home doing nothing for four weeks. Lola had to keep a close eye on him, so he doesn't overdo it, they got to the Fashion House and everyone was so glad to have him back. Stefan's employees loved him; they all said he is a fair boss. Stefan's personal assistant came into the office to remind Stefan about his eleven o'clock meeting with the designers from New York. The personal assistant had ignored Lola's instructions to check with her about Stefan's diary and Lola wanted to know why? Stefan's personal assistant responded and said she is Stefan's personal assistant and she should be the one managing Stefan diary. Lola then shouted at her, don't give me attitude or you will manage yourself out of a job. Stefan's personal assistant was about to respond when Stefan cut in by announcing he is in the room. He asked his personal assistant to leave his office, and he also confirmed he will be at the eleven o'clock meeting. The personal assistant walked out of the office looking very proud of herself because she got her own way. He told Lola not to treat him like an invalid, and that he can chair his meetings. Lola told him he shouldn't even be at work today let alone attending meetings. They both sat in silence Stefan was reading his emails and Lola was just sitting there fuming. After catching up with all his emails, Stefan got up to go to the meeting. 'Are you coming darling?' Asked Stefan. 'What's the point? You don't listen to anything I say,' Lola replied. 'The point is, you will upset my personal assistant by being there and you can take control of the meeting as you always do, Lola, stop being childish, I know you have my best interest at heart, but you can't have slagging matches with the staff, you must remain professional at all times,' said Stefan. 'I will not apologise to her, but I promise not to behave like that again,' replied Lola. Stefan pulled her towards him and told her she is such a stubborn little madam; count your lucky stars I love you.' He kissed her on the lips; she kissed him back. I love you too Stefan. Stefan pulled away from her, 'you know I can't resist you stop trying to seduce me in the office,' he said. 'You are the one trying to seduce me;' she replied. 'Let's go to this meeting and then we are going home, I don't feel well,' he said. Lola smiled at him, she knew what that meant.

The following week, Lola got a call from Alhaji informing her he would only stopover in London for one night, he is in transit to America. Lola went to see Alhaji at the Hilton Hotel on Edgware Road. Alhaji was waiting for her in the hotel's restaurant. 'It's been a long-time Lola,' he said. 'I know, I have missed you so much, I thought you were staying for a while? Asked Lola. 'No, not this time, my meeting in New York was re-scheduled, so I can only spend the night in London,' Alhaji replied. 'Have you spoken to Mark,' she asked? 'Yes, he picked me up from the airport,' replied Alhaji. 'I have tried to call him, but he is not returning my calls,' said Lola. Alhaji told Lola to stay away from him and not to bother to call him again. Lola told Alhaji that she has fallen in love with Stefan, but she wanted to remain friends with Mark. Alhaji asked Lola to promise to stay away from Mark and not to contact him again. She didn't understand why Alhaji was warning her off Mark, but Mark hadn't tried to get in touch with her anyway, so she promised not to contact him. Alhaji and Lola had dinner and talked all evening about her relationship with Stefan and everyone in Lagos. It was getting late and Lola had to leave. 'I will see you in Lagos for the Christmas holidays, tell Alhaja that I will see her soon,' said Lola. 'How long are you staying in New York for?' Asked Lola. 'I will be there for a week,' replied Alhaji. Lola gave Alhaji a big hug, and he told her he will leave first thing in the morning, she asked him to call her as soon as he arrives in New York to confirm his arrival, she wished Alhaji a safe journey, the lady from reception came over to tell her that the taxi she called was outside.

Lola's mother had spoken to Alhaji about the fact that Mark had been dating Lola, but he had refused to take the genotype test. Lola’s mother wanted Alhaji to talk to him since Alhaji was like a father to Mark. Alhaji called Mark and asked him what his intentions were towards Lola. Mark told Alhaji that, he was in love with Lola and he wants to marry her. Alhaji asked if Lola had told him she has the sickle cell trait. Mark said she did, but from his understanding, there is no issue because he doesn’t have the trait and if they were to have children, the child would not have sickle cell anaemia, the worst that could happen, is that their child would inherit the sickle cell trait from Lola. Alhaji then told Mark that he found out that his father died of complications of sickle cell anaemia. Mark was finding it difficult to believe what Alhaji was telling him, he remained quiet. 'Hello, are you still there?' Asked Alhaji. 'Yes, I am still here, are you sure my father had sickle cell anaemia?' Asked Mark. 'Yes, I am Mark,' replied Alhaji.

Alhaji told Mark that he went to see his father’s wife, and she told him that Mark's father's family kept the fact he died of complications of sickle cell anaemia a secret. Mark's father was very healthy, however, when he was younger Alhaji remembered he was always sick and he was always absent from school. Alhaji would take all the school homework to Mark's father's house, so he didn’t fall behind. That is how they became best of friends, despite all the time missed at school, Mark's father still passed all his exams. Alhaji told Mark that his father came to London on business and that is when he met Mark's mother, he would always complain about the cold weather in London, he wanted Mark's mother to move to Nigeria, so he didn’t have to spend too much time in London. Mark's mother had just started the Estate Agency, and she believed she would have lost all the money she had invested in the business if she had sold it back then. Mark's father caught the flu on his last trip to London; the flu was untreated. When he returned to Nigeria, his condition got worse, the doctors in Nigeria treated Mark's father for Malaria, having sickle cell anaemia caused complications, he never recovered; the autopsy put the cause of death has pneumonia. Alhaji told Mark that he needs to go for a genotype test; Lola has already had her fair share of heartache with sickle cell anaemia. Alhaji also said they can still have a relationship, but they both need to talk about the implications of having a child with the sickle cell blood disorder, something Lola already knows too well. They both have a boy and a girl between them, so having children is not a priority. Mark couldn't believe what Alhaji was telling him, he didn't know his father had sickle cell anaemia, he told Alhaji that he will do the test, but if he has the trait, he cannot be in a relationship with Lola because he still wants children of his own. Mark's baby's mother is always trying to keep his daughter away from him and he wouldn't be able to deal with the death of a child. Alhaji told Mark to talk to Lola about how he is feeling. Mark told Alhaji that Lola doesn't care how he is feeling, she is too busy caring for her boss, to worry about his feelings. Alhaji asked Mark to promise he would talk to Lola. Mark promised that he would talk to Lola and thanked Alhaji for all his advice. 'I will see you in London next week,' Alhaji said. 'Please call when you arrive, I will come and pick you up from the airport,' said Mark. 'Thank you, my son, your father would have been so proud of you, Goodbye Mark.' 'Goodbye Alhaji.'

Mark did the genotype test the very next day, the test showed he had the sickle cell trait; he was so disappointed. Mark decided that he will not speak to Lola again, he called Alhaji in Lagos and told him the results of the text, he also told Alhaji that he will break the promise he made to him. Mark had no intention of speaking to Lola about his genotype test result, he wants nothing to do with Lola anymore, she had already moved on.

Stefan's cast was removed after six weeks; his arm has healed. Stefan was taking Lola to meet his mother in Italy, his father had died two years ago, of a stroke. No one understood why he died, he was very healthy, and he didn't seem depressed. Stefan came from a very large family he had four sisters and two brothers. Apart from Gianni and his youngest sister, the rest lived in Italy, Stefan's youngest sister lived in America. Stefan wanted to spend Christmas in Italy, but, Lola had already made plans to spend Christmas in Nigeria. Stefan arranged for them to have an early Christmas in Italy, his family were looking forward to meeting Lola. Lola was so nervous and excited at the same time about meeting Stefan's family.

Stefan had an early morning breakfast meeting with a client who had flown in from New York. He was up and getting ready. Lola was awake, but she wasn't feeling too good, she had been up half the night throwing up. Lola ended up sleeping in one of the spare rooms because; she didn’t want to disturb Stefan knowing that; he had an early start in the morning. Stefan was looking for Lola; he didn’t even realise that she was not in the bed. He shouted out to her. 'Lola, where are you?' 'I am in here;' she replied. Stefan put his head around the door, 'what are you doing in here?' Asked Stefan. 'I was feeling sick during the night; I didn’t want to disturb you, so I came in here,' she replied. 'What is the matter?' he asked. 'I don’t know; I think I have the flu.' replied Lola. 'You need to see the doctor, it’s not normal to be throwing up. I will cancel the breakfast meeting and take you,' said Stefan. 'No, I will book an appointment and take a taxi to the doctor's surgery, I am feeling much better now,' Lola said. 'I know I have that effect on people, but I want you to promise to see the doctor this morning,' said Stefan. 'I promise,' Lola replied. She was checking Stefan out; he looked very handsome in his Gianni Versace tailored suit. Stefan always looked good in everything he wore, but this morning he looked so sexy. Most Italians men are well-dressed and they always wear good shoes. Lola can’t stand men who wear horrible shoes. 'My darling, please text me when you have seen the doctor,' said Stefan. 'Will do, I will be at the Fashion House after I have seen the doctor,' replied Lola. 'Why don’t you stay at home today?' Asked Stefan. 'I have lots of work to do and I am feeling much better now.' Lola said. He kissed her on the forehead; 'I haven't got time to argue with you this morning. I will speak to you later.' He told her he loved her, and Lola said she Loved him more. At eight o'clock Lola called the doctor's office, her appointment is at ten o'clock. She got ready; the doctor's surgery was just a ten-minute drive from the Fashion House. The doctor checked Lola over, everything seemed to be fine. He then asked her when she had her last period. Lola told him it was a month ago, he asked her to do a pregnancy test. 'I can't be pregnant, I am on the pill,' she said. Lola did the test anyway; the results showed she was five weeks pregnant. Lola was in shock. The doctor asked her if its good news? 'I don't know; I need time to get my head around it,' Lola replied. Lola left the doctor's office, the doctor told her to stop taking the pill if she is thinking of keeping it. Lola is in shock; she was wondering how this could have happened? She forgot to take the pill just one day while Stefan was in the hospital. Lola walked hoping she would have decided what to do before she got to the Fashion House. When she arrived at the Fashion House, she was more confused than ever, she sat in Stefan office, knowing he would call her any minute from now, he knew the appointment was ten o’clock because she had sent him a text. Lola’s phone rang, Stefan name flashed up. 'Hello, my love, what did the doctor say?' Asked Stefan. 'Stefan, I am pregnant.' Lola replied. 'Are you? Who is the father?' Asked Stefan. Lola was getting angry; she wasn’t expecting that response. 'You are, how dare you,' she shouted down the phone. 'Lola, calm down, I was just joking,' he said. 'Well, don’t joke about something as serious as this, I am still in shock and I am still trying to figure out how it happened,' said Lola. 'Lola, do you need me to tell you about the birds and the bees?' Asked Stefan. 'Stefan, can’t you be serious for one second?' Asked Lola. 'Why should I be serious?' You are having my baby; I am thrilled about that. Lola are you not happy?' Asked Stefan. 'I don’t know how I am feeling, I am still in shock,' replied Lola. 'I have finished my meeting and I am on my way back to the office, when I get there, you can explain why you are not over the moon about the fact that you are carrying my child,' said Stefan. Stefan put the phone down without giving Lola a chance to respond. Forty-five minutes later Stefan walked into his office; Lola was sitting at his desk. He smiled at her and walked up to her; he pulled her up out of the chair and threw his arms around her and gave her a big kiss on the lips. 'Are you going to keep this baby?' He asked. 'I haven't thought about that;' she replied. 'What is there to think about?' Asked Stefan. 'I love you and I have enough money to support you and the baby, I will ask you one more time, are you going to keep the baby?' Asked Stefan. 'Yes,' Lola replied. Stefan pulled her towards him and kissed her. 'You have made me the happiest man in the world, we are going home to celebrate,' said Stefan. 'What about the meeting at three o'clock?' Asked Lola. Stefan pressed the intercom; it went through to his personal assistant. 'Cancel my three o'clock,' said Stefan. Stefan took his figure of the button as his personal assistant was speaking. He grabbed Lola's bag off the table and pulled her towards the office door. Stacey came running out of the office, 'what am I going to tell the client, the reason for the cancellation?' She Asked. 'You are my personal assistant are you not?' 'Yes, I am,' replied Stacey. 'Then do your job, Stacey,' replied Stefan. Stefan then took Lola's hand and walked out of the Fashion House. The driver was too busy flirting with the receptionist; he didn't notice Stefan and Lola standing at the Fashion House entrance door. Stefan shouted over to the driver. Tony, get the car, we are going home. The driver turned around and replied, 'Yes boss'. The driver pulled up and Lola and Stefan got into the car.

As soon as Stefan got into the house, he went to the cellar and took out one of his best wines, he brought it to the lounge where Lola was sitting, he put two glasses on the table and went to the kitchen and came back with some orange juice. Stefan poured a big glass of wine for himself and poured the orange juice into the other big glass for Lola, she gave him a disapprovingly look. 'I can have a small glass of wine you know,' said Lola. 'Who told you that? When did you become a doctor?' Asked Stefan. 'You drink the orange juice and I will celebrate with the wine,' said Stefan. 'I am allowed at least one glass of wine in my condition,' Lola replied. 'Get it in writing, until then enjoy your orange juice,' said Stefan. 'Lola, are you happy about having my baby?' Asked Stefan. 'Yes, I am, I was in shock when I first heard the news but, I am getting used to the idea, it would be nice for Temi to have a little brother or sister. I need to call my mother and give her the good news,' said Lola. 'Wait a minute young lady as he pulled her back down, we have not finished celebrating yet,' he said. 'Stefan, you have been celebrating for the both of us, you have finished a whole bottle of wine, said Lola. Stefan smiled at her and said, 'Come here this is something we can both do together' he said. He pulled Lola towards him and kissed her neck. Lola loved it when he did that to her, he unzipped her dress from behind and then he unhooked her bra exposing her breast. Stefan then put her nipple in his mouth. Lola was moaning with pleasure. Stefan stood Lola up and took her panties off. He then laid her back on the couch and ripped off his own clothes. Stefan got on top of her and caressed her breast and kissed her, he told her he loved her, and he is happy that she is in his life. Lola told him, she was so lucky to have him and that, he has made up for all the turmoil she has had in her life, she believes God has given her a second chance and she is so thankful. Lola was just about to say something else and he kissed her and caressed her body with his hand, he put his figures between her legs and she was moist, he was teasing Lola, so she put his penis inside her. They made love twice. Stefan fell asleep holding Lola close to him. Lola lay awake, just thinking how lucky she was to have Stefan. Stefan woke up and pulled her closer. Lola was so eager to get up and call her mother, she got up, he asked her where she was going, I need to call my mother, he mumbled something and closed his eyes again. Lola went into the other room and came back with a throw to put over Stefan's naked body.

'Hello, mother.' 'Hello, my daughter, how are you?' She asked. 'I am okay mother, how's Temi?' Asked Lola. 'He is fine, he will soon be back from school,' Lola's mother replied. 'What is the matter, my daughter?' Lola's mother asked. 'Nothing mother,' she replied. 'There must be something wrong for you to be calling me now,' she said. 'Nothing is wrong; I am calling you to give you my good news, I am pregnant with Stefan baby,' said Lola. 'Oh my God, congratulation my daughter, I am so happy for you, when did you find out?' Asked Lola's mother. 'I found out this morning, I am five weeks pregnant,' replied Lola. 'How did Stefan take the news?' Asked Lola's mother. 'He is even more excited than I am,' she said. 'Are you and Stefan still coming over for Christmas?' Asked Lola's mother. 'Yes, we are, we are also going to Italy to see his family next week, Lola told her mother. 'This is fantastic news, I will tell Temi that, he will soon have a brother or sister,' said Lola's mother. 'Do you think he will be pleased about that?' Asked Lola. 'Yes, he will, Temi is always asking if he can have a brother or sister like his friend next door,' Lola's mother replied. 'Bless him,' replied Lola. 'Have you heard from Mark?' Lola's mother asked? 'No, I haven't, I have stopped trying to get in touch, I tried to get in touch several times but, he kept on ignoring my calls. I will not call him again unless he returns my call,' replied Lola. 'Mark as the sickle cell trait,' Lola's mother said. Lola was silent. 'Hello, are you still there?' Asked Lola's mother. 'Yes, I am, no wonder he his ignoring my calls, did he do the test?' Asked Lola. 'Yes, he did, Alhaji convinced him to do the test. Mark's father died from complications of sickle cell anaemia,' Lola's mother told Lola. 'Oh, my God, it's a good job we didn't continue the relationship, he was so adamant he didn't have the sickle cell trait and the fact he didn't want to discuss the implications of having a child with the sickle cell blood disorder,' said Lola. 'Well, you don't have to worry about that anymore, you are having a baby with Stefan and white people don't inherit sickle cell anaemia, Lola's mother said. 'Mother, that is not the point, there are lots of people out there who will fall in love with each other and they will break up because they both have the sickle cell trait. I would not have broken up with Mark if he had the trait, he refused to talk about the financial and emotional

implications of bringing up a child with the sickle cell blood disorder,' Lola said with anger in her voice. 'Lola, get your head out of the clouds, Mark told Alhaji that he wanted nothing to do with you because; he doesn't want a child that will inherit the sickle cell blood disorder, I didn't tell you before because, I thought you were over his friendship,' Lola's mother responded. 'How can someone turn off their feeling for someone they claim to love,
over something that may or may not happen?' Asked Lola. Lola pretended not to be concerned about what her mother had just said. 'Are you okay Lola? Don't let what I said upset you. I didn't intend to tell you about Mark but, I couldn't let you go on thinking you owe him anything. I won't let you waste your energy on someone that is not worth it,' said Lola's mother. 'I am okay mother, is that Temi I can hear in the background?' Lola changed the subject. 'Yes, he is back from school,' replied Lola's mother. 'Let me please talk to him,' said Lola. Lola's mother put Temi on the phone, Temi told his mother about school and his friend next door. Lola felt good hearing her son's voice, she told him he will soon have a little brother or sister. Temi was overjoyed and said he would tell everyone in his class. Lola told him to keep it a secret for now.

'Temi, do you know how to keep a secret?' Asked Lola. 'Yes, I do' he replied. 'Good boy,' she replied. Temi asked for a new bike, Lola asked him why he needed a new bike, Temi told her the old bike's brakes are not working, she told him she will ask Grandma to take the bike to get the brakes fixed, she told Temi that it's a waste of money buying a new bike now but, she promised to buy Temi a new bike once he moves to London, she told him there was a massive park where he could ride his bike. 'Okay, mummy,' he replied. 'Give the phone to Grandma please,' she said. 'Bye-bye mummy.' 'Bye Temi, mummy loves you.' 'I love you too,' Temi replied. Lola’s mother came back on the phone, 'can you tell the driver to fix the brakes on Temi’s bike, please?' Asked Lola. 'Yes, I will do that my daughter,' replied Lola's mother. 'I will speak to you later. Goodbye mother,' 'Goodbye my daughter.'

Chapter Ten

Lola tossed and turned all-night, she was so nervous about meeting Stefan's family in Italy. They were getting ready to go to Heathrow Airport. Stefan is excited about visiting his family in Italy; he was looking forward to showing Lola off to the family. Gianni and his family are meeting Stefan and Lola at Heathrow Airport. Lola and Stefan arrive at Heathrow, Gianni and his family had checked in already. After greeting each other the Italian way, kissing on both cheeks. Gianni wanted to know why they were both late. 'It was Lola's fault,' Stefan said. 'No, it was Stefan's fault, he didn't tell me it's winter in Italy; I thought it was hot all year round,' said Lola. Gianni's wife then butted in and told Lola and Stefan to check-in, so they could all sit together on the plane, 'you can both continue this argument after check-in,' she said. They all laughed at what Gianni wife said. Stefan and Lola checked in, it wasn't a full flight, so they all got seats in the same row.

They arrived at Palermo International Airport after a one hour and thirty-five-minute flight from Rome Airport. They had a four-hour wait in Rome, so they went shopping to while away the time. Stefan mother lives in Castellammare del Golfo it was only a twenty-minute drive from the Airport. Stefan's driver flew out yesterday, he picked them up at the Airport.

Stefan's mother was waiting for them at the window, as soon as she saw the range rover come through the gates. She shouted to everyone and ran out to the driveway; she was excited to see Stefan and Gianni. They were hugging and

kissing, then Stefan's mother noticed Lola and Gianni's wife. She hugged Gianni's wife and gave her the traditional kiss on the cheeks. Then Stefan was talking to her in Italian, he was introducing Lola to her, Stefan's mother's eyes lit up, she said bonito, which means beautiful. Stefan's mother hugged her and kissed her on both cheeks, she was now shouting for the rest of the family to come and meet Lola. Stefan whispered in Lola's ear, 'She likes you,' said Stefan. That made Lola feels good, she wasn't sure if Stefan's mother would like her. Lola made a good impression on the family, they all thought Stefan's had made a good choice. They were all seated in front of the fire in the lounge talking and catching up on lost time. Stefan's mother was sitting next to Lola, and she turned around and said to her in Italian that, Lola should never break her son's heart. Lola looked at Stefan for translation. Stefan looked embarrassed; it was Gianni that told her what his mother had said. 'My mother wants you to promise you will never break Stefan's heart,' said Gianni. Lola turned to Stefan's mother and nodded her head to confirm she wouldn't. Stefan's mother got up to go to the kitchen, all the women got up too. Gianni's wife beckoned to Lola to follow. The smell of the food coming out of the kitchen was making her hungry. The food was ready, there were so many people around the family table. It was such a big dining room; it's used for all family occasions. Stefan was one of three boys and he also had three sisters. All their partners and children were present. You would think it was a party setting and not just one big family reunion. Lola let her guard down, they all seemed to like her. Stefan's younger sister lives in Atlanta and she married an African American, who owns a music production company.

The following day Stefan hired a minibus for them to take a road trip to Palermo City.

Palermo City is one of the largest cities in the Mediterranean and it's now among the top tourist destinations in both Italy and Europe. The forty-five-minute ride was too much for Lola; she was sick a few times along the way. Everyone soon realised that she was pregnant, and they were all excited about the news. Stefan's mother was singing and thanking God for returning her son's happiness. The family all knew Stefan was suffering from depression. Stefan tried to pretend he was okay, and he refused to see anyone about it, his mood swings were clear to the people close to him. His family noticed the change in him and they knew it was down to Lola. They arrived in Palermo and they drove around the City showing Lola the sites, this was for Lola's benefit; everyone else had seen the sights before, the children seem very excited to see them again. They drove past the Palermo Cathedral, Palazzo Del Normanni, Teatro Massimo and the Politeama Theatre. Stefan and his family couldn't decide which restaurant they should go to, they ended up going to Al Cascinari, the owner is an old family friend. Stefan's mother was not happy, she wanted to cook for all the family but, everyone wanted to eat out, she then decided, if she must eat out, it will be at her old family friend's restaurant. The antipasti and fish were delicious. They stayed at the restaurant for three hours eating and talking. Stefan knew Lola was getting tired, he caught her several times dozing off, he whispered in Lola's ear, "I am sorry honey; I know you are sleepy, we are leaving right now". Lola nodded in agreement. Stefan is always considerate of her feelings, he made sure she wasn't left out. Stefan's mother doesn't speak English so; he became her interpreter. They all got on the minibus and headed back to Castellammare del Golfo. The journey back didn't seem that long. When they arrived at Stefan's mother's house, Lola excused herself; she had a shower and went to bed. She was so tired; it had been a long day. Stefan came up to make sure she was all right. 'Lola are you okay,' he asked? 'Yes, I am Stefan, I am just tired; I can't keep my eyes open, spend time with your family,' she said. 'You are my family,' said Stefan. That made Lola feel so good, to hear him say that. 'Stefan, I love you so much,' she said. 'I love you too,' he replied. Stefan gave Lola a passionate kiss on the lips. 'I know you are sleepy, so I will let you be, Goodnight my darling,' he said. 'Goodnight Stefan,' she replied. Lola's alarm went off at six o'clock, even though it was seven o'clock in Italy. Stefan stirred, 'why have you still got that damn alarm on?' He asked. 'I am sorry; I forgot to disable it,' she replied. Don't give me attitude young lady he said as he pulled himself on top of Lola. 'I have so missed you; we have not been alone since we got here,' Stefan said. Stefan kissed her neck; he put his hand up her nightdress, he was searching for her breast, he felt them and pulled the nightdress over her head and sucked on her nipple. Lola was moaning, Stefan knew what to do to turn her on. Stefan continued to tease her, 'I know the real reason you put the alarm on, so you can have your wicked way with me, you Jezebel,' said Stefan. Stefan put his figures between her legs, she was wet, and he went inside her with ease. After making love, they both got up and went for a shower and then they went down for breakfast. Stefan's mother was already preparing breakfast for everyone. They both went into the kitchen to greet her, Stefan's mothers kissed them both on the cheeks then directed them to the dining table she put all the food she had made on the table. There was freshly made orange juice, assorted fruit, pancakes, bacon, sausages and boiled eggs or scrambled eggs. Lola helped herself to pancakes and fresh orange juice, she also had one of Stefan's mothers Frittelle Crema, they were so delicious. The rest of the family joined them at the dining table. You could smell Stefan's mother's breakfast throughout the house. After breakfast, Stefan told Lola that they were going for a drive alone. Lola said she didn't think it was a good idea for them to wander off alone. 'I thought this holiday was for you to spend more time with your family?' Asked Lola. 'Yes, you are part of my family now,' said Stefan. 'You know what I mean,' replied Lola. Lola was getting frustrated with his sarcastic manner. 'Lola, I know what you mean, there's no need to get upset, I want to spend time alone with you,' replied Stefan. 'I am not upset; I am just trying to understand how your mind works,' replied Lola. 'Well, no one is paying you to think,' said Stefan. Stefan gave Lola a passionate kiss on the lips, to stop her from saying anything else. He picked up the picnic basket, took her by the hand and directed her towards the range rover. Gianni and the driver were standing outside, Stefan shouted over to Gianni and said, they will meet the rest of the family later that evening at La Timpa. Gianni nodded and told them to have a great time. 'Where are you taking me anyway?' Asked Lola. 'I am taking you to the place; I used to go as a young child,' replied Stefan.

Stefan and Lola drove on the A29 highway connecting Palermo to Trapani. Just metre away from the A29 Stefan pointed at the ruins of Segesta. This is where I and my family would come during the summer; we watched the productions staged here. Lola wanted to know why the temple had no roof, he told her they built the temple to impress the visiting Greek diplomats, but when the Greek diplomats left, the town's people didn't even bother to finish the temple. Stefan and Lola took the food basket Stefan's mother had made for them down to the temple, he took out a bottle of sparkling non-alcoholic wine and poured it into the glasses. He gave one glass to Lola, and they ate the sandwiches. Lola took another sip of her wine and she then noticed something in the glass, she poured out the rest of the wine and realised that there was a ring in the glass, she tipped the glass to get hold of the ring, it was a diamond ring. Lola looked at Stefan with a surprised looked on her face, by this time Stefan was on one knee asking her to marry him. Lola's eyes filled with tears, she knew Stefan loved her, but she never in a million years thought he would want to marry her. Lola said yes to Stefan proposal, and he picked her up and kissed her. 'Thank you, Lola, you have just made me, the happiest man alive,' he said. 'You have just made me the happiest woman alive,' replied Lola. 'Now I wish I had made this proposal somewhere more private,' said Stefan. 'Why? This is such a beautiful and romantic setting,' replied Lola. 'I know but, now I want to make love to you, I am so turned on, it hurts,' said Stefan. Lola smiled at him. 'You have always got sex on the brain,' said Lola. 'That is the effect you have on me and that is why you love me,' replied Stefan. They both sat down and continue to eat their lunch. It was getting chilly, so they went back to the car. They took a selfie together. Stefan said the temple is now, even more special, it will always remind me of when I was a youngster and it's the place where I proposed to my future wife. Lola smiled at the thought of being Stefan's wife, she couldn't believe she almost threw it all away.

All the family were waiting at the restaurant, as soon as Stefan's mother saw Lola, she ran up to her and checked her left hand, she was overjoyed when she saw the ring on Lola figure. The rest of the family congratulated them. Stefan's family knew Stefan would propose to Lola, the meeting at La Timpa was for a congratulatory dinner party. Stefan's twin sons were also at La Timpa.

They arrived from London that morning, Lola had met Stefan's sons several times, and they all got on well with each other. The twins knew Lola made their father happy, and that was all that mattered to them, the twins lived with their mother. They both were in their final year in college studying Law. The party went on until eleven thirty. Lola was getting tired, So Stefan told the driver to drive them home. Stefan had been drinking, the driver would come back for everyone else. Stefan's mother went home with Stefan and Lola, she was tired and tipsy. When they got home, Lola and Stefan had a quick shower and went straight to bed. Stefan woke up in the middle of the night and woke Lola up. 'Are you awake?' He asked. 'I am now,' replied Lola. 'I need to congratulate you,' he said. 'For what?' Asked Lola. 'For agreeing to put up with me,' replied Stefan. 'What are you talking about?' Lola asked half asleep. 'I am a hot-blooded Italian and I want what is mine,' he said. He pulled Lola towards him. 'Can't you wait until the morning?' Lola asked. 'No way, I will still want what is mine in the morning too, don't deprive your future husband of what belongs to him,' Stefan replied. Stefan caressed her breast; he knew how to turn her on, she could never resist him when he sucked on her breast. Lola was groaning. 'Do you want me, Lola?' he asked. 'Yes, I do,' Lola replied. Lola was just wearing a T-shirt. He put his figures between her legs and she was wet, he pulled Lola on top of him and she went to work on him, Stefan was about to come so, he switched positions. They both climaxed together, they talked for a little while and then they fell asleep.

The next couple of days went so fast, everyone was getting ready to go back to their various normal lives. Lola and Stefan had such a wonderful time in Italy, all the family wanted to do it again for Christmas, Lola and Stefan had to decline the offer because they were both going to Nigeria for Christmas. Gianni and his family, the twins were flying back to London with Stefan and Lola. Stefan's youngest sister and her husband will take a later flight back to America. The rest of the family lived in Italy. Stefan's mother cried when Stefan got into the minibus, everyone in the family knew Stefan was her favourite child, Stefan being in love again gave her so much pleasure, she hated the twins mother for making her son unhappy. That was one of the reason's she didn't come to Italy with the twins, the other reason was that Stefan didn't want her there. Stefan wanted nothing to ruin the early

Christmas family gathering. Lola had met Stefan's former wife before and she came across as rude. Stefan's former wife came to drop off the boys one weekend. Lola said hello to her, but she ignored her. Stefan refused to come out of his room to see her. His former wife asked the twins to call their father, but he told his sons to tell their mother to put whatever she wanted in writing. That infuriated his former wife. She then turned to Lola and said, 'I wish you luck with misery guts. 'Lola told her they didn't need luck, they love each other, and that they are both happy.' Stefan's former wife took one scornful look at Lola and stormed off and slammed the door behind her.

Even though Lola was glad to be home, it was also great to see Stefan so relaxed and happy in Italy. Lola didn't allow Stefan to take any work-related phone calls, and she had warned his personal assistant that, if she calls him for any work-related issues, she would sack her. Stefan was in his study on the phone to his personal assistant, catching up with everything that had gone on while he was away, his personal assistant had done a good job of keeping on top of things, Stefan's personal assistant doesn't like Lola, and the feeling is mutual. Stefan personal assistant hated the idea Stefan was dating Lola but, deep down she knew Lola was the best thing that could have happened to him, Stefan changed when Lola joined the company.

The boys were in the basement playing table tennis. Lola called her mother and spoke to Temi. Temi was so excited when Lola told him; she will see him in two weeks' time. She had not seen her son for six months. 'What do you want for Christmas Temi?' She asked. 'Can I have a new computer game, please?' Asked Temi. Lola had already brought him an iPad, he can download all the games he wants from it, she didn't tell him about the iPad, she wanted to keep it as a surprise. One of his friends at school had one, even though he never asked for one, Lola knew he would love an iPad. Temi would never ask for anything just because his friends had it, he was always happy to share his toys with the children in the neighbourhood; sometimes he would just give them away to any child that had no toys. He is such a sweet little boy, always thinking of others. After speaking to Temi for a while, her mother came on the phone. She told her mother that Stefan had asked her to marry him. Lola's mother was dancing and singing. 'Fantastic news, my daughter, I hope you said yes?' 'Yes, I did,' Lola replied. 'Are you going to get married in Nigeria?' Asked Lola's mother. 'No, Stefan has a big family and they all want to be at the wedding, we have agreed to get married in the summer in Italy. I will ask Alhaji to give me away,' said Lola. 'That is an excellent idea, he has been a good father figure to you, how I wish your father was still alive,' said Lola's mother. 'I wish he was still alive too, I miss him so much,' replied Lola. 'Have you heard from Mark?' Lola’s mother asked. 'Yes, he sent me a text, he wanted to know how I was, I didn’t reply to his text. After what he had said to Alhaji, I have nothing to say to him anymore,' said Lola. 'I don’t blame you, my daughter, his words were so hurtful,' replied Lola's mother. 'I wanted to stay friends with Mark, but, I can’t be his friend not after what he said about me, he couldn't have had any feeling for me if he could turn off his feelings for me so easily,' said Lola. 'Don’t worry my daughter; God has given you a man that will love you no matter what, you can’t blame Mark for his ignorance. The lack of awareness is a disease on its own,' said Lola's mother. 'That is so true mother, I have two things to look forward to the birth of my baby and my wedding to Stefan, I will not let Mark put a damper on my happiness. Mother, I must go now, it’s time to cook dinner. I will speak to you tomorrow.' 'Goodbye, my daughter.' 'Goodbye, mother.'

Lola cooked dinner for Stefan and the boys. Stefan’s mother had taught Lola how to cook spaghetti carbonara the way Stefan liked it. 'This is delicious Lola, it even tastes better than my mother’s, don’t tell her I said that,' they all laughed.

After dinner, the twins went to watch a movie in their room. Lola and Stefan were in the lounge trying to book their tickets to Nigeria online. The twins also wanted to go to Nigeria, but their mother put a stop to that. 'The boys are spending Christmas with me,' the twins mother demanded. 'It’s up to the boys, not you,' replied Stefan. The twins’ mother was screaming down the phone. 'Damn you, Stefan, don’t turn my boys against me like you have turned everybody else against me,' the twins mother shouted. The twins agreed to spend Christmas with their mother; she had no one apart from her husband to spend the Christmas with, her husband’s family don’t like her, they didn’t want him to marry an older woman who would never bear him any children. Stefan told Lola that his former wife's husband would leave her, he was only ever with her for the money. His former wife was a successful accountant in a London City Law firm, she also had a generous divorce settlement from Stefan. The twins told their father that their mother was unhappy and that she and her husband argued all the time, their mother spent most of her time at work, she hardly saw the boys, they wanted to move in with their father, but she would not allow it. The twins are looking forward to leaving home, they are both going to Harvard to study Law.

Lola and Stefan are travelling to Nigeria tonight, they were both excited, Nigeria was the place they first met. Stefan thought Lola was an ignorant little madam, she was late for their meeting and she never completed the contract. Alhaji ended up completing and signing the contracts on her behalf. Stefan didn't realise at the time that; she had lost her first child. They got to the Airport, they had already checked in online, they had to weigh their baggage, as per usual, Lola had packed everything, but the kitchen sink. She spent months going shopping buying things for everyone in Nigeria. When she thought she had shopped for everyone, she would remember someone else. Virgin Atlantic charged her one hundred and forty pounds each for two extra bags, they are both entitled to three bags each as they were travelling upper class. Out of the eight bags, only one of them belonged to Stefan. Lola and Stefan finished checking in and went to relax in the Virgin Clubhouse after all the hustle and bustle at check-in, Stefan needed a drink. Lola was feeling peckish, so she ordered a light meal. They were in the Clubhouse for about an hour when the concierge announced that it was time for boarding. After take-off, Lola prepared herself to go to sleep, she turned her seat into a bed and drifted off to sleep. Lola was so tired; she had been running around all day doing all the last-minute stuff both at home and at work. Stefan was the sensible one; he left everything for his personal assistant to do, Lola is a perfectionist, she is not happy unless she is doing or supervising things herself. Stefan was not only going to Nigeria for pleasure; he was also meeting new clients in Abuja. So, this time, there were no instructions from Lola for the personal assistant not to get in touch. In fact, it was paramount that she stayed in touch.

They arrived at Murtala Muhammed Airport the following morning. Lola's mother and son Temi were waiting in the arrival hall. Temi was so eager to see his mother. Temi was up half the night; he kept getting up in the middle of the night to ask his grandmother what time it was. Lola and Stefan didn't take too long collecting their baggage's, the good thing about travelling upper class is that your baggage will always come out first. Two porters assisted them with their baggage, the porters took the baggage to their parked minibus. As soon as Temi clapped eyes on his mother, he ran to her. Lola swept him into her arms and was kissing and cuddling him, Temi refused to let go of her. She had missed her son so much; she didn't realise how much she had missed him until he was in her arms.

Lola's mother was greeting Stefan; she couldn't get a hug from her daughter because Temi refused to let her go. Temi went over to question Stefan, so Lola then could greet and hug her mother. The driver led the porters to the car, has the porters were returning to the arrival hall, Stefan gave them both ten pounds each, the porters appreciated his generosity. Lola's mother complained that Stefan had given them too much money, she was calculating the exchange rate in her head. Stefan told her not to worry, he will not lose sleep over twenty pounds. They got into the minibus and headed to Lagos Island, Lola was glad to be back in Nigeria, everyone is always in a hurry to get somewhere, the only thing Lola didn't miss was the long traffic jams. Although, when you are sitting in an air-conditioned car, you don't feel it as much. Lola's mother was updating her daughter about everything that had been going on, even though, half of what her mother told her was things she had already told her over the phone. Stefan was not a stranger in Lagos; he has been coming to Nigeria off and on for ten years. Stefan is familiar with his environment, he even understands and speaks broken English. It took two hours to get from the Airport to Victoria Gardens. Stefan had never been to Lola's house, he was so surprised to see how beautiful her house is, he had been to so many beautiful houses in Lagos, Stefan has his eye on a mansion in Banana Island. 'Is this your house, Lola?' Asked Stefan. 'Yes, Alhaji gave me this house as a wedding present,' she replied. 'Alhaji is such a generous man,' replied Stefan. 'He sure his, he is like a father figure,' said Lola. 'He is coming round this evening, I called him to tell him we were arriving today, I am looking forward to seeing him again, he is a good friend of mine. I would never have met you if it wasn't for him,' said Stefan. Lola was unpacking while Stefan, had a shower, Lola's mother and the housekeeper were cooking breakfast. Temi was sitting at the breakfast table waiting for his mother to come downstairs. Lola kissed him on the head and then sat beside him. Temi kept questioning Lola, he wanted to know when he was leaving to go to London, Lola told him he would have to wait until the summer, it was too cold right now in London. Lola had a lazy Sunday at home; she has so much to do in the three weeks stay in Nigeria. Stefan and Alhaji are going to Abuja tomorrow to meet their new clients. The clients wanted to make a good impression so, they paid for the airfare and hotel accommodation in Abuja.

In the evening Alhaji and his wife came to visit, it was so nice to see them both again. Alhaji's wife was fussing over Lola as usual; she is so happy that Lola and Stefan are getting married next year after having their baby. It was such a lovely evening just chatting with old friends. Tunde's sister also came round; they had bumped into her at the Airport, she had just arrived from Dubai. Tunde's sister had moved to Abuja not long after Tunde's death. Lola even got a surprise phone call from Tunde's mother. Tunde's mother said she would come to Lagos on Tuesday to see her. Lola has forgiven Tunde's mother for all the horrible things she said and did to her while Tunde was alive, she was not willing to hold on to any bad feelings towards her, she is Temi's Grandma and Lola loves her new life, she believes things happen for a reason. The evening went so well, Stefan and Alhaji were busy chatting about business. Alhaji is going with Stefan to Abuja to meet the new clients. The new clients had come all the way from Thailand, Alhaji knew the Nigerian Directors but had never met the Directors from Thailand. This would be a good opportunity to meet with them and to make sure that Stefan got the best business deal. Alhaja and Lola's mother were organising Lola's wedding, Lola went along with everything they said just for a quiet life. Unknown to them, the wedding ceremony will take place in Italy. The one thing that was definite is that Alhaji, Alhaja and her mother would be attending. It's just going to be a small ceremony with close family and friends. Alhaji got up and announced it was time to go. 'So Soon?' Asked Lola. 'Yes, Stefan and I have an early start in the morning, the driver and I will be here to pick you up at eight in the morning,' Alhaji told Stefan. 'I will be ready, unlike some people; I am always on time,' said Stefan. Lola gave Stefan a stern look; she knew Stefan was referring to her.

Not long after Alhaji and Alhaja left, Stefan went to bed he needed an early night, he had a few drinks too many. He could feel a headache coming on, he took painkillers, had a shower and went to bed. Lola stayed up a little longer with Temi and her mother. They were planning Christmas food shopping, in Nigeria, you could never tell who would turn up on Christmas day, there is no such thing as a guest list so, to be on the safe side, it's always good to cook as if you are expecting the whole neighbourhood, food never goes to waste in Nigeria. First thing in the morning they will go to the meat market.

It was eight o'clock on the dot and Alhaji was sitting in the car. Alhaji's driver sounded the horn of the car, Stefan was up and ready to go, he kissed Lola goodbye, and she hugged him and told him to stay safe. Lola asked Stefan to call her as soon as they arrived in Abuja, Lola felt uneasy about Stefan flying to Abuja, he promised to call as soon as the plane lands. Lola hugged him again and refused to let go. Stefan had to pull himself away. 'Lola everything will be okay,' he said. She wished them both a safe flight.

Lola, Temi and her mother got ready to go to the meat market, she was not herself until two hours later, when she got a phone call from Stefan, to say they had both landed in Abuja. The rest of the day Lola spent going from one meat seller to the other. Lola also bought four live Chickens, for their Christmas day feast. By the time, they got home, Lola was so exhausted, she had something to eat and had a shower. She then curled up on the sofa and watched African Magic with Temi. It was so nice to not have to lift a figure and do anything, there were people around ready to run errands for you, something she had missed in London. If you want things done in London, you had to do it yourself. After watching two movies, both Temi and Lola were sleeping on the sofa. Lola's mother woke them both up and told them to go to bed.

Lola woke up the following morning to the sound of the phone ringing, she could hear the excitement in Stefan voice. 'I guess the meeting went well?' Asked Lola. 'It sure did, it went better than I expected. I have just won a ten-year deal with the Thai company; they liked my proposal, Alhaji executed it very well. We will be back tomorrow; we are all going to dinner tonight with the Minister of Tourism,' Stefan said. 'That's fantastic, I hope you all have a good evening, don't drink too much, I don't want you coming home with a sore head,' replied Lola. Stefan said he couldn't promise anything, but he would do his best to come home in one piece. 'What are you doing today?' Asked Stefan. 'I am having a duvet day, Tunde's mother is coming round later, I am guessing she will spend the night. I know she will have lots of gossips to tell me. It will be a gruelling afternoon/evening, I must put on a brave face, said Lola. 'Don't worry my love; it will be over before you know it,' Stefan said. 'I doubt that somehow, she is spending the night, her daughter will pick her up tomorrow afternoon,' replied Lola. 'Don't stress about it too much, it will be over before you know it,' he repeated himself. 'That's easy for you to say over in Abuja, getting drunk and delirious, said Lola. 'I have got to go now; I am running out of credit,' said Stefan. 'Stefan, not that old chestnut again?' Lola replied. 'Love you,' said Stefan, and he disconnected the phone.

Lola got up, to prepare for Tunde's mother's arrival. Lola didn't want her former mother-in-law to have anything to moan about, the cook was preparing Tunde's mother's favourite dish honey beans and plantain. It was quite nervy

meeting Tunde’s mother again; she had aged so much. After Tunde’s death, she became very depressed, and she had a minor stroke.
Tunde's sister took her mother to stay with her in Abuja to help with her recovery, she recovered from the stoke but, her speech is affected,
she was all apologetic about the way she had treated Lola, Lola felt nothing but pity for her. Even though Lola had forgiven her, it was impossible to forget. Lola told her she had forgiven her, she told Tunde’s mother that, all that had happened to her in the past was her destiny and not all her doing. Tunde’s mother cried, Lola put her arms around her and begged her to stop. Tunde’s mother kept begging for forgiveness. Lola told her she had forgiven her a long time ago. Lola told her she was expecting a baby and that, she will re-marry after the birth of her baby. Tunde’s mother prayed for Lola and wished her well, then she got up to leave. She asked Lola if it would be okay with her to visit her grandson anytime she was in Lagos. Lola said it would be okay. Tunde’s mother gave Temi a big hug and then left, she had refused to stay and eat. The whole experience was exhausting for Lola, it brought back feelings she had buried. Stefan called, hearing his voice made her feel much better. 'I will be home in an hour,'

Stefan said. 'I have missed you,' Lola replied. Stefan asked her what was wrong, he could tell she was not her usual cheerful self. 'I am okay, I had a visit from Tunde's mother,' replied Lola. 'I hope she didn't upset you again?' Asked Stefan. 'No, she didn't, I am just tired,' replied Lola. 'How's the wedding perpetrations going?' Asked Stefan. 'I am sure it's going well, I am not involved in the preparations, my mother, and Alhaja seemed to have it all under control,' replied Lola. Stefan laughed and told her to stop being facetious. 'Okay, honey, I will be home in an hour,' he said. 'I can't wait,' Lola said. Then the phone went dead.

The Christmas holiday in Nigeria has ended, and they both had a wonderful time, mixing business with pleasure is not ideal but, it worked for them this time. Lola and Stefan were getting ready to go back to London, she felt so guilty having to leave her son behind. Temi was trying so hard not to cry. Lola gave him a big hug and told him, she will see him in London during the summer holidays. Lola was due to give birth in June and the plan was to get married in July. Temi and her mother would be in London on both occasions.

First day back at the fashion house Stacey, Stefan's personal assistant was standing chatting with the receptionist. Happy New Year Stacey shouted towards Lola. Lola responded in the same manner, she knew Stacey didn't like her and she suspected that Stacey fancied Stefan. She never confronted Stefan about her suspicions, she knew one day she would find out the truth. Stacey was just about to ask a question, then Stefan walked through the door. Her face lit up, and she went over to wish Stefan a happy new year. She kissed him on both cheeks, this infuriated Lola, but, she dared not show it. Stefan took Lola by the arm and they walked towards his office. Stacey shouted out to Stefan, our meeting is in fifteen minutes, Stefan ignored her. Stefan's bad manners pleased Lola this time. Everyone in the fashion house was used to Stefan's moods, it even took Lola a while to get used to them. Stefan kissed Lola on the lips and asked if she would join him for lunch. Lola said she would and then they both went to their separate offices.

Lola looked at herself in the mirror, she was showing, she was not ready to tell anyone at the fashion house she was pregnant. Ever since the workers at the fashion house learned of her relationship with Stefan, they treated her like an outsider. Stacey treated her with so much contempt. Stacey would be livid if she found out that Lola was pregnant and planning to marry Stefan. Lola was still looking at her stomach when Stacey barged through the door. She took Lola off guard; 'can't you knock,' Lola shouted at Stacey. 'Sorry' shouted Stacey. 'I only came to cancel your lunch date with Stefan, we are out together all day,' she said. 'Well, I am sure Stefan could have told me that himself, now please leave my office,' shouted Lola. 'How was the business trip to Nigeria? Did things not work out the way you wanted?' Asked Stacey. Lola could feel herself filling up with rage. 'Who told you that my trip to Nigeria was a business trip?' Asked Lola. 'Well, Stefan implied it was,' Stacey replied. 'Stacey get out of my office before I throw you out,' shouted Lola. 'I am leaving, keep your hair on,' replied Stacey. Stacey left and slammed the door behind her. Lola is angry and finding it very difficult to fight back the tears. What was Stefan playing at, Is he ashamed of our relationship? Many thoughts were going through her mind. Lola knew she had to get out of the office, she wanted no one to know Stacey had got to her. Lola called a cab, she wasn't sure where she wanted to go, but, she was angry at

Stefan and she wanted to get out of the fashion house. She walked towards the reception area and she could see Stacey and the receptionist laughing and smirking at each other so she pretended to be on the phone and walked straight past them both. The cab driver asked her where she wanted to go? Lola didn't have a clue. After five minutes, she told the driver to take her to Oxford Street. She went bridal shopping, Lola's eyes were filling up with tears, she had just realised that she didn't have a close friend. Shopping for a wedding dress is something you do with your friends. Lola had remained cordial with the people at the fashion house, but she wasn't close to anyone there.

After spending two hours in the bridal shop and still not able to decide on a dress. She left and went to Selfridges to have lunch on her own. As she was walking through the makeup department, a lady approached her and asked her to come and get her makeup done. Lola looked at her and thought why not, it wasn't lunch time yet, so she might as well while away the time having her makeup done, she had never had her makeup applied by a professional before, so, she thought it a good idea to do so. Lola sat in the chair, her phone rang, it was Stefan, Lola ignored it and let it go to voicemail. Stefan left a message, asking where she was, he had been to look for her in her office. No one knew where she was. Stefan had cancelled the meeting he had because he was not feeling too well.

Lola got talking to the lady doing her makeup, she found out that the lady is from Nigeria and her name is Ada. It was Ada's lunch break now, so they both went to lunch at The Henry Holland around the corner from Selfridges. Ada recommended the chilli con carne. It was delicious. Lola enjoyed her lunch break with Ada, they were talking about their time in Lagos. Ada had lost track of the time, Ada glanced at her watch and shouted, 'oh my God, my boss will sack me for being late.' Lola gave Ada her card, and she said, 'If he does, you can come and work for me as my personal assistant.' 'I might take you up on that offer,' replied Ada. They both walked back to Selfridges. Ada told Lola that she had enjoyed their luncheon and hopes they can do it again soon. Lola told her to call her when she is next available, and that she would love to meet up with her again. They said their goodbyes.

Lola called a cab and told the driver to take her to the fashion house, she was feeling much better now, and she would allow no one to ruin her mood. Lola had put her phone on silent mode because Stefan had called her several times. She put the volume back on and listened to the voice messages. Lola asked the driver to take her home. Stefan was in bed asleep when she got home, he had taken cough medicine, which had made him drowsy. Lola could not make any sense of what he was saying so, she allowed him to sleep. Lola pulled the leather recliner chair close to the bed and sat and watched Stefan sleep, she felt guilty for not answering his calls, after a while, she also fell asleep.

Stefan woke up about two hours later, he called out to Lola. 'Stefan, how are you feeling? I can't believe I fell asleep too,' said Lola. 'I am okay, I am coming down with a cold, my throat is sore, replied Stefan. Lola got up and went to make Stefan some lemon and honey. Lola left the bedroom and came back five minutes later with the hot water, lemon and honey. 'Thank you, my darling,' said Stefan. 'Why did you leave the office without telling no one where you were going?' Asked Stefan. 'I didn't want to interrupt your meeting, I planned to call you later, but I lost track of the time,' replied Lola. 'Where were you?' Asked Stefan. 'I went to Selfridges for some retail therapy,' replied Lola. 'Trust you, Lola, I am dying, and you go shopping,' said Stefan. Lola scorned at Stefan joke. 'Lola, I am just joking, what is wrong with you today?' Asked Stefan. 'Nothing is wrong with me, it must be my hormones all over the place,' replied Lola. Stefan asked Lola to lie down beside him. Lola then asked Stefan when are they going to announce their engagement? Stefan said not just yet. Lola wanted to know why she could feel herself getting angry again. Stefan said he has his reasons. 'Are you ashamed of me?' Asked Lola. 'Don't be silly Lola, I don't want to talk about this anymore,' replied Stefan. Lola was trying so hard to hold back the tears, she couldn't help feeling that Stacey had something to do with the reason, he didn't want to announce their engagement.

The following morning, Stefan seemed to have recovered from his sore throat. The hot water with lemon and honey seemed to have done the trick. They both arrived at the fashion house. Stefan's former wife was sitting in Stefan's office with two other men, she recognised one man, he was their client from China. Lola didn't know who the other man was. Stacey and Stefan's former wife were sitting there chatting, they must all be acquaintances. Lola entered the office and greeted everyone in the room, offered them complimentary drinks and nibbles, then she excused herself, she didn't want to be at the meeting. After about fifteen minutes, Stacey, and Stefan's former wife left Stefan's office, and they both headed to Stacey's office. They were in the office for over an hour. Stefan and the two gentlemen emerged from his office. Stefan popped his head around Lola's office door and told her they were all going to lunch, he looked pleased with himself. The deal is complete, and the contract signed. Stefan said he was trying so hard to stay cool. 'Do you want to come to lunch with us?' He asked. 'Is your former wife going too?' Asked Lola. 'Yes, she is part of the deal breaker,' said Stefan. 'In that case, I will pass this time,' replied Lola, and she gave him the look. Stefan recognised the look and decided not to confront her about her jealousy. 'I will see you at home later,' he said. 'How long is this lunch?' Asked Lola. Stefan closed the office door, he didn't want to argue with her, his new business partners were standing in the hallway. Lola sat at her desk, she was furious with herself for letting her jealousy get the better of her. She was also angry at Stefan for dismissing her like that. She could feel the rage building up inside her. At that minute her phone beeped, it was a WhatsApp message from Ada inviting her to lunch. Lola and Ada have been messaging each other by text and WhatsApp, she liked Ada a lot. Lola sent Ada a message confirming lunch at one, she put the matter with Stefan to the back of her mind, she will deal with Stefan's arrogance when she gets home. She finished replying to all the emails in her inbox, they had built up while she was on holiday. Lola went to the post room and on her way back, she bumped into Stacey in the hallway. Lola ignored her, Stacey shouted across to Lola, 'have you got a problem with me?' 'You are paranoid,' Lola replied. 'Lola, I believe you have a problem with me,' Stacey repeated herself. Lola told Stacey that, she couldn't help her with her paranoia. Stacey was about to say something but, Lola cut in and said, 'she didn't have time to talk right now because she was going out for lunch, have a good afternoon Stacey.' Lola hurried passed her into her office. Stacey was left standing in the hallway gobsmacked, she was expecting Lola to have a full-blown argument with her, she couldn't believe Lola just dismissed her like that. Stacey was so angry; she was just about to knock on

Lola’s office door when Lola opened it. 'Sorry, I can’t stop now, I am late for my lunch date,' said Lola. 'Just because you are getting married to Stefan doesn’t mean you are the Queen B around here,' said Stacey. Lola stopped for a minute, smiled and then walked out of the building. Lola felt smug, she now knew the news of her marriage was all over the fashion house and that was the reason Stacey was being bitchy towards her. Stacey and Stefan’s wife are close friends. Stefan’s wife must have told Stacey they are engaged. Lola wondered who told Stefan’s Wife but, deep down, she couldn’t care less.

Lola and Ada had a lovely lunch at a Chinese restaurant in Soho. Ada had started a new Facebook Page. After talking to Lola about sickle cell anaemia, she was so desperate to help create awareness of sickle cell anaemia. Ada had heard about sickle cell anaemia but, she didn’t know enough about the blood disorder. Lola is glad Ada is taking an interest in creating sickle cell awareness. Ada was talking about fundraising and for the money to go towards sickle cell awareness. Ada invited Lola to a friend’s wedding, she had bought ten yards of Ankara and she asked Lola to sew outfits for them both. Most of the friends of the bride will wear the same Ankara print. Ada insisted that their outfit must stand out from all the rest of the ladies that will wear the Aso Ebi. Aso Ebi is the material friends and family wear so they look the same. Lola was looking forward to the party, she had not been to a Nigerian wedding party since she moved to London. Lola asked Ada to meet her at the fashion house tomorrow so, she could measure her for the party outfit and to choose a design. They went back to Selfridge; Ada was going back to work while Lola went shopping for shoes. She had no intention of going back to the fashion house, Lola didn't want to face Stacey, she didn't want to say anything to her, she might later regret. She wanted to speak to Stefan first. Stefan wanted no one in the fashion house to know they were engaged or the fact she is pregnant. Lola decided that she would find out why.

It was late in the evening when Lola got home. Stefan was sitting in the kitchen drinking a bottle of wine, Lola could tell by his demeanour he was angry. 'Where have you been?' Stefan shouted out to her. 'I was out shopping with my friend Ada,' replied Lola. Who is Ada and why have you been ignoring my calls again?' Asked Stefan. Lola replied and told him it was because she was angry with him. 'What's wrong with you?' Asked Stefan. 'Nothing is wrong with me, what the hell is wrong with you Stefan?' Asked Lola. 'You want no one to know we are engaged or I am pregnant, are you ashamed of me?' Asked Lola. 'What are you talking about Lola? I am not ashamed of you, the only reason I asked you not to tell anyone about our engagement and that you are pregnant was due to the business meeting I had today with my former wife and her business contact. The business deal went through today, so you can announce our engagement on BBC News if you want to, my former wife is a very vindictive person, and I thought if she knew, she would put a stop to the business deal in China. Lola, why would you think I am ashamed of you? I love you and I don't care who knows it,' said Stefan. 'Your wife knows about our engagement and so does Stacey, Stacey congratulated me today and your former wife couldn't even look at me,' said Lola. 'Lola, I am so sorry, my sons told their mother because she was organising a holiday to Florida in August. They had no choice but to tell her that, you and I were getting married in August. She was so angry, she tried to call off the deal with her business client. She backed down when Mr Chuna threatened to cut her out of the business deal. Lola, I am so sorry, I told her about the baby today,' said Stefan. 'Stefan, you are such a cold and calculating person, everything you do has a reason behind it. How could you weigh our relationship on a business deal? What would have happened if the business deal fell through because of me?' Asked Lola. 'Lola, stop being childish, I took a calculated risk, it would have made no difference if I lost the deal. I love you, we are getting married, and I can't wait to be a father again. 'Lola why are you making a big deal about this?' Asked Stefan. 'Lola could feel the rage building up, I am not being childish, I am not your trophy wife, you can't treat me like you own me. I am off to bed, you can sleep on the sofa,' said Lola. 'There you go again acting like a child, instead of us talking about this, you are running away. Goodnight Lola, I will enjoy sleeping on the sofa. I have spent many nights on the sofa,' said Stefan. 'Sweet dreams,' shouted Lola. 'When you start acting like an adult, then we can talk,' replied Stefan. Lola was in bed tossing and turning, she had cried herself to sleep, now she is wide awake going over all what Stefan had said to her. How dare he call me a child? Lola realised that she had not had dinner. She could hear her tummy rumbling. Lola got up and made her way to the kitchen. There was leftover Jollof rice in the fridge. As she walked past the living room, she popped her head around the living room door. She saw Stefan lying down on the sofa. Lola was about to close the living room door Stefan shouted out, 'tea please.' 'Make it yourself' Lola shouted back at him.

Lola was in the kitchen warming her Jollof rice in the microwave. Stefan came into the kitchen and asked her if there was enough rice for him too. Lola dished more rice for Stefan, she hated fighting with him. They both sat at the dining table in the kitchen and ate their rice in silence. When they both had finished eating, Lola put the dirty dishes in the dishwasher. Stefan was sitting at the dining table; he was pouring a glass of wine for himself. Lola walked over to him, 'I am so sorry Stefan, I don’t know what came over me this evening.' Stefan kissed her on the forehead and told her to say no more. 'You had the right to be angry, Lola, I am so sorry for not putting your feelings first. Can you ever forgive me?' Asked Stefan. 'I have forgiven you already, I hate it when we fight,' said Lola. 'Me too, I hate the sofa even more,' said Stefan. They both laughed as they headed towards their bedroom.

Stefan’s engagement and the fact that Lola was having his baby seemed to be the talk of the fashion house. Everyone was congratulating Stefan, the only person who congratulated Lola was the receptionist and Lola believes she only congratulated her because Stefan was standing beside her.

Lola spent the afternoon designing hers and Ada’s outfit for Ada's friend's upcoming wedding. Stacey didn’t think their relationship would last, Lola being pregnant and marrying Stefan came as a big shock to her. Lola couldn’t care what anyone thought about her and Stefan, her relationship with Stefan was rock solid and they both loved each other.

Chapter Eleven

Lola and Ada are getting ready for Ada's friend's wedding. They both looked stunning in their outfits, the outfits are a perfect fit. Ada helped Lola with her makeup. Stefan knocked on the bedroom door. 'Are you two not ready yet?' Asked Stefan. 'We are ready,' replied Lola. 'The driver is outside waiting for you both,' said Stefan as he walked out of the bedroom door, he looked back and said, 'You both look stunning and you could pass for twins.' 'Thank you, Stefan,' they both replied at the same time. 'You see what I mean? You even have the same thoughts,' he laughed and left the room. Lola had that disapproving look in her eye. Lola had just finished wrapping her head tie then she tied Ada's head tie for her. The bridal head tie is in fashion and Lola is an expert at head wraps. 'Which car are you guys taking?' Asked Stefan. 'It doesn't matter,' replied Lola. 'You better take the Range Rover; not sure your head gears will fit in the Bentley,' said Stefan. 'Stefan, you are in the wrong job, you ought to be a comedian,' said Lola. 'Don't wait up, this party is going on until the early hours of the morning,' said Lola. 'You make sure your back here before midnight,' replied Stefan. 'I will see what I can do,' replied Lola. 'Bye my darling, don't miss me too much,' Lola said. 'No chance of that, I am going out with the lads,' replied Stefan. 'Stefan is so funny,' said, Ada. 'Don't encourage him,' replied Lola. Lola kissed Stefan and told him she was missing him already. Stefan smiled at Lola. 'See you later honey,' he shouted after her.

Lola and Ada arrived at the venue off the Old Kent Road, the venue is on an industrial estate. It was impossible to get to the venue with all the doubled parked cars that were blocking all the entrances of all the buildings along the road. It's a good job Lola didn't need to find a parking space. The driver dropped them off as close as he could, they had to walk the rest of the way. Lola instructed the driver to come back and pick them up at eleven o'clock. Inside the hall, it's full of people, Ada's friend who is getting married is a socialite, and she is well-known in Nigeria and in London. Ada's friend lives in Nigeria but, she is always in London on business, she told Lola that, her friend's husband is a younger man and owns a successful real estate agency here in London, she didn't like her friend's husband because he didn't treat her friend right. Ada was so surprised when her friend told her they were getting married out of the blue. Lola didn't attend the church wedding because she had morning sickness. The hall was so hot, Lola saw an invitation on the table she was sitting at so, she picked it up to fan herself with it. She saw a familiar face on the invitation card, looking back at her it was Mark's face. Lola couldn't believe her eyes. Lola wanted to get out of there, she knew she had to come up with a good excuse to leave the party. At that moment the bride and the groom came into the hall, she saw Mark and looked away. Ada got up and danced towards the bride and groom, they stopped and danced with Ada for a few minutes. Mark then noticed Lola, he smiled and hurried his bride to the front of the hall. Lola wanted to leave, she had not seen or spoken to Mark since the day Stefan was admitted in hospital in a coma. Ada was having so much fun; she didn't want to ruin it for her. Lola got up, 'Ada I am just going to make a phone call,' she said. 'Do you want me to come with you?' Asked Ada. 'No, I will be back in a minute,' replied Lola. Lola went outside, and she called Stefan. 'What's the matter, Lola?' Asked Stefan. Stefan could tell she was stressed, she was talking too fast and not making any sense. 'I need you to come and pick me up.' shouted Lola.

'I can’t, I have been drinking,' replied Stefan. 'Lola, what’s the matter?' Stefan was getting worried, he thought something had happened to her. 'I need to get out of here,' Lola replied. 'Are you not enjoying yourself?' Asked Stefan. 'No, I am not, I can’t believe I am at Mark’s wedding,' she replied. Mark's wedding? What’s the problem? Are you not happy he is getting married? Asked Stefan. 'That’s a stupid question, Stefan. I don’t believe it’s proper for me to be at his party uninvited,' replied Lola. 'Lola, you are overreacting, I will call the driver and ask him to come and pick you up, he will text you with a time of his arrival, I am at the club with the lads so, I will see you later. I will try to get away early,' said Stefan. He was being dismissive. 'Don’t hurry home, I don’t want to ruin your evening just because I had a bad evening,' Lola said. 'That’s true, you will see me when you see me,' said Stefan. 'You can be a right arsehole sometimes Stefan,' said Lola. 'Lola, I was just joking, loosen up, it’s not the end of the world,' replied Stefan. By this time, Stefan was angry, he told her he would speak to her later and cut off the phone. 'How dare he hang up the phone on me?' she was speaking out loud. Lola was just about to call him back when someone tapped her on the shoulder, she turned around it was Mark.

'Hello, Lola,' said, Mark. 'Hello,' replied Lola. 'Did you come with Ada?' Asked Mark. 'Yes, I did, I didn't know you were the one getting married,' said Lola. 'Didn't Ada show you the invitation?' Asked Mark. 'No, she didn't, she talked about your wife a lot, she never spoke about her friend's husband,' said Lola as she tried to justify herself for being at his wedding. 'Why are you out here?' Asked Mark. 'I am waiting for my driver,' replied Lola. 'Are you leaving already?' Asked Mark. 'Yes, I must go,' replied Lola. 'Why do you have to go? Come back in and enjoy the party, you don't have to leave on my account,' said Mark. 'I am not leaving on your account, I am not feeling too good,' replied Lola. 'There you are, I was wondering where you got to, I didn't know you knew Mark? Asked Ada. 'Yes, we are old friends, we haven't seen each other for a long time,' said Mark. 'Everyone is looking for you, it's time to cut the cake,' said Ada. 'Okay,' said Mark, he turned to Lola and said speak soon. Lola just nodded. 'Are you okay Lola?' Asked Ada. 'No, I need to go home, I am not feeling well,' replied Lola. 'Lola, you were okay, half an hour ago, I hope this has nothing to do with Mark? I hope he was not rude to you? I don't like him, he thinks he's God gift to women,' said

Ada. 'No, he wasn’t rude. I didn’t know it was Mark’s wedding, I wouldn’t have come if I knew he was the one getting married,' said Lola. Lola told Ada that she and Mark had a brief relationship and the only reason they broke up was that he refused to take the genotype test and worst of all he refused to talk about the possibility he might have the sickle cell trait. Ada was surprised, she told Lola that her friend told her that Mark had made her have a test while she was in Nigeria, at the time she thought it was odd but, it makes sense now. 'Does your friend have the trait?' Asked Lola. 'No, she told me she has the AA blood type,' replied Ada. If your friend has a baby with Mark, the child could only have the trait and not sickle cell anaemia,' said Lola. Lola didn't think it was her place to tell Ada that Mark has the trait. Lola received a text message, it read I will be outside in thirty minutes, she told Ada that she was going home and wanted to know if she should send the driver back to pick her up at eleven. Ada told her not to worry, she will hitch a ride with her friend who lives around the corner from her. Lola kissed Ada on both cheeks and thanked her for her understanding. 'Let me make it up to you, let’s have lunch on Wednesday?' Asked Lola. 'Yes, I will like that, I will text you on

Wednesday to tell you what time my lunch break is,' replied Ada. 'That will be great,' said Lola. 'Bye Lola' said Ada. 'Enjoy the party,' replied Lola.

As soon as Lola got home, she was on the phone with her mother. 'Hello Mother, guess what?' Asked Lola. 'What's the matter, my daughter?' Asked Lola's mother. 'Do you remember I told you I was going to a wedding?' Asked Lola. 'Yes, my daughter, I thought it was today?' Asked Lola's mother. 'It is today; I have just got home from the party. 'What's the problem?' Lola's mother asked. It was Mark's wedding, I didn't go to the church in the morning because, I was feeling sick, but, I was at the party and that was when I realised who was getting married. 'Oh my God, was Mark surprised to see you?' Asked Lola's mother. 'I think he was, it was awkward for the both of us and you won't believe who he got married to,' said Lola. 'Who did he marry?' Asked Lola's mother. 'He married Bella the socialite,' Lola replied. 'Are you serious?' I know Bella's mother, I went to her granddaughter's funeral four years ago,' said Lola's mother. 'What was her granddaughter's cause of death?' Asked Lola. 'Complications of sickle cell anaemia,' replied Lola's mother. The word sickle cell anaemia shot through Lola like a bullet. 'Bella's brother has sickle cell and his daughter died of sickle cell anaemia,' said Lola's mother. 'Oh, my God, sickle cell anaemia is so common among Africans and there's still so much ignorance surrounding the disorder, no one wants to talk about it. Nigeria has the highest population of people with sickle cell anaemia,' said Lola. 'I wonder if Bella got tested for sickle cell anaemia?' Asked Lola's mother. 'Yes, she did, Mark made her take the test before they got married,' replied Lola. 'I wonder why Alhaji didn't attend the wedding? I will call him in the morning and ask him, I will let you know what he says,' said Lola's mother. 'Thank you, mother, I feel much better talking to you, I felt terrible not telling Ada that Mark has the sickle cell trait,' said Lola. 'My daughter, Mark is no longer your problem, you have your own wonderful life, so just concentrate on your life. Did you tell Stefan?' Asked Lola's mother. 'Yes, I did, he is angry with me for overreacting,' replied Lola. 'Lola, I keep telling you about your temper, make sure you make up with Stefan, you must not argue over Mark with Stefan, Lola's mother said. 'Okay, mother, I will make it up with him as soon as he gets home,' said Lola.

It was past midnight when Stefan got home, he didn’t want to face Lola, he couldn’t understand why Lola reacted the way she did when she realised she was at Mark’s wedding. Stefan was wondering if Lola still had feelings for Mark. Lola was sitting in the living room when he got home. 'Hi, Stefan,' said Lola. 'Hello Lola,' Stefan said. 'Honey, I am so sorry, the shock of being at Mark’s wedding made me overreact, If I knew beforehand, I would have dealt with the situation much better. I don’t have feelings for Mark, it was awkward being there, I am glad he’s now married, I love you and nothing will come between us. I am so sorry I called you an arsehole, I didn’t mean it,' she said. 'Let’s talk about this in the morning,' Stefan said. 'No Stefan, I don’t want to go to bed with this on my mind, you always like to bottle things up, let’s talk about it now. I will not sleep unless I know you have forgiven me,' said Lola. 'Lola, I am not angry with you. I am just too tired and drunk to talk about it now, I promise we will talk in the morning,' said Stefan. Lola knew there was no point in arguing with Stefan when he was like this, Lola had no choice but, to let him go to bed.

Stefan was in the shower when Lola woke up, 'Good Morning Stefan,' she said. 'Morning, my love,' replied Stefan. 'How are you feeling today?' Asked Stefan. 'I am okay, why didn't you wake me?' Asked Lola. 'You tossed and turned half the night so, I thought I should leave you to sleep,' replied Stefan. Stefan got out of the shower, I have left the shower running for you,' he said. 'Thank you, I need to talk to you about last night,' said Lola. 'If it's about Mark, I don't want to talk about him, you were angry because you were at Mark's wedding reception without your knowledge. I don't know what you want to talk about, are you still in love with Mark?' Asked Stefan. 'Hell no,' shouted Lola from the shower. 'How can you even think I still have feelings for Mark?' Asked Lola. 'Okay, if Mark had invited you to his wedding would you have gone?' Asked Stefan. 'Maybe,' replied Lola. 'So, what is your damn problem? Asked Stefan. There isn't one, I know I am being silly,' replied Lola. 'What's new? replied Stefan. Lola had to bite her lip, she promised her mother she would not let Mark come between her and Stefan. Lola changed the subject, why are we up so early this fine Sunday morning,' Asked Lola. Have you forgotten? We are taking the boys to Silverstone today,' replied Stefan. 'No, I haven't forgotten, I thought we were going in the afternoon,' said

Lola. 'We need to leave early to beat the Sunday traffic on the M1,' said Stefan.

It was the twin's birthday Thursday gone, Stefan had bought tickets for them to watch Motor Racing at Silverstone. It should be a lovely day out, Stefan had purchased VIP hospitality tickets and they also get to meet Lewis Hamilton. 'I am going down to start breakfast; do you want bacon and eggs?' Asked Stefan. 'Yes, please,' replied Lola. Stefan is a fantastic cook, he always said, if he wasn't in the designer business, he would have been a chef. Lola came down in her dressing gown. 'What time are the boys getting here?' Asked Lola. 'They should be here anytime from now,' replied Stefan.

The twin's arrived just after ten, their mother dropped them off, the boys were so excited to be going to Silverstone, they were looking forward to meeting Lewis Hamilton. 'Are you not ready yet?' shouted, Stefan. 'I am ready; I can't decide which shoes to wear,' replied Lola. 'You have more shoes than Russell & Bromley,' replied Stefan. 'You should have been a comedian Stefan,' said Lola. 'Hurry, we will be late,' said Stefan, he was getting irritable. 'Okay, I am ready now,' she said. Lola was wearing a lovely brown dress with white dots and a hat to match. You look gorgeous, you remind me of Julia Roberts in that movie, what's it called?' Stefan asked the twins. 'Pretty Woman,' the boys shouted out at the same time. 'What are you saying, I look like a prostitute?' Asked Lola, Stefan and the boys burst out laughing. 'Who is the comedian now?' Asked Stefan. 'Hello boys, how are you? I hope you had a great birthday on Thursday?' Asked Lola. 'It was okay, good old Dad is making up for it today though, thanks for our birthday presents, as you can see we have the trainers on today, Lola, I bet you chose them, they are super cool. Dad has good taste, but, he is not as Trendy as you,' said the boys. 'Is it pick on Dad today? Come, let's go, we will be late, said Stefan. Lola turned to the twin's and said, 'you are both welcome.' It took almost an hour to get out of London but once they got on the M1, the motorway was free of traffic. They had a fab day at Silverstone, the best part was meeting Lewis Hamilton, they took pictures with him and they also got his autograph. Even Lola and Stefan took a picture with Lewis Hamilton. It was late in the evening when they got home. Stefan had to drop the boys off first, Lola was so tired, she had so much fun, but, she had worn herself out. 'Do you want something to eat?'

Asked Stefan. 'No, I am stuffed, I need to have a shower, then I am off to bed,' replied Lola. Lola was just about to get into the shower and the phone rang. Stefan shouted up to her, 'your mother is on the phone.' 'Please tell her I will call her tomorrow, I am too tired to talk,' said Lola. Lola could still hear Stefan on the phone to her mother. Lola knew he was having trouble reassuring her that everything was all right. When Lola got out of the shower, there was a missed call on her phone. It was Ada, she had left a message asking Lola to call her back. Ada had called in the morning too; she was getting worried that she had not heard from Lola. Lola had never ignored her calls before, Lola sent Ada a text message telling her she will call her tomorrow, that she was too tired and that she is having an early night. Ada texted back and said okay.

Stefan was running late, he's attending a meeting up in Manchester at eleven o'clock, his driver called to say he is stuck in traffic, Stefan had to take a taxi to Victoria Station. 'See you later Lola, I will call you when I am on my way back,' said Stefan. 'Good luck Stefan, I hope the meeting goes well,' said Lola. 'Me too,' replied Stefan. The driver arrived and took Lola to the office. The receptionist was so chatty this morning, asking her how she was and if she had a good weekend. Lola remained civil, she wasn't in the mood for niceties. Stacey popped her head around Lola's office door. 'Do you know what time Stefan will be back? He is not answering his phone,' said Stacey. 'I am sure he will call you back when he is ready,' replied Lola. 'So, do you know when he is coming back or not?' Asked Stacey. 'Or not,' replied Lola. Stacey gave her a blank stare and closed the door behind her. Lola loved getting under Stacey's skin. At that moment the phone rang, it was Ada. 'Hello Ada, I was just about to call you,' said Lola. 'Oh, really?' Asked Ada. 'Yes, I was, I am so sorry about Saturday,' said Lola. 'That's okay Lola, I got a lift home with my friend, she only lives around the corner. Lola are you going to tell me what freaked you out?' Asked Ada. 'Let's meet for lunch and I will tell you all about it, replied Lola. 'Okay, I will text you to confirm what time my lunch is today,' said Ada. 'Great, see you later,' said Lola. While Lola was on the phone to Ada, her mother had called so, she called her mother back. 'Hello Mother,' said Lola. 'How are you, my daughter?' replied Lola's mother. 'I am okay, how are you?' Asked Lola. 'I am also doing okay,' replied Lola's mother. 'How's Temi?'

Asked Lola. 'He is doing okay too, he has gone to school,' replied Lola's mother. 'He has been ticking off the dates on his calendar, he can't wait to come to London,' said Lola' mother. 'Bless him,' replied Lola. 'Did you speak to Alhaji?' Asked Lola. 'Yes, I did,' replied Lola's mother. Lola's mother told Lola that Alhaji wasn't invited to Mark's wedding because, he was the one who suggested that, Mark's wife should get tested for sickle cell anaemia. Ella's family were furious with Alhaji and so was Mark, he insulted Alhaji, he called him an interfering old fool. Alhaji was so angry, he doesn't want to even hear Mark's name. 'My daughter, thank God, you had a lucky escape,' said Lola's mother. 'I have had a traumatic experience with sickle cell anaemia, I don't think I could go through it again, having a baby with Stefan, I don't have to worry about sickle cell anaemia. The worse thing that could happen is that my baby has the sickle cell trait,' said Lola. 'That is so true my daughter, I thank God for Stefan,' said Lola's mother. Lola and her mother spoke for a while longer. 'I must go now, I have done no work since I got here, please go to the shop and see the manager, he said he was having a problem with one seamstress. I am thinking of selling the business, there will be no point me keeping the business in Lagos when you and Temi move over here,' said Lola. 'Don't be hasty my dear, the business in Lagos is doing so well,' said Lola's mother. 'I know mother,' said Lola but, I am thinking of going into real estate, that is where the money is nowadays,' said Lola. 'That is also a good idea my daughter, a friend of mine was talking about properties at the Beechwood Estate at Aja. If you are interested, I will ask for the details, my friend said it's a great investment,' said Lola's mother. 'Thank you, Mother, I am interested, and I know Stefan will be too, I will speak to you tomorrow; I have so much work to do. Bye Mother,' said Lola. 'Goodbye, my daughter.'

It was already ten forty-five and Lola had done nothing all morning, she was just about to read her emails and her phone rang, it was Mark. She didn't want to talk to him after finding out how rude he was to Alhaji, Lola picked up the phone. 'Hello Mark, congratulations,' said Lola. Thank you,' replied Mark. 'How are you?' Asked Mark. 'I am tired of being pregnant apart from that, I am fine,' said Lola. 'My wife is pregnant too,' he said. 'Congratulations, you are a fast worker, I hope she took the test for sickle cell anaemia?' Asked Lola. Yes, she did, she did the test in

Nigeria and she does not have the trait,' said Mark. 'Well, that is great news,' replied Lola. 'Have you spoken to Alhaji?' Asked Mark. 'Yes, I have,' lied Lola. 'So, did he tell you we had a misunderstanding?' Asked Mark. 'Misunderstanding, that's an understatement, you were damn well rude,' replied Lola. 'Well, he should learn not to interfere in my business,' said Mark. 'He had your best interest at heart,' replied Lola. 'I knew you would side with Alhaji,' said Mark. 'It's not about taking sides, it's about telling the truth, what if we had got married, and I was carrying your baby, how would you feel knowing your child could have sickle cell anaemia?' Asked Lola. 'It's only a fifty-fifty percent chance,' replied Mark. Is it a fifty-fifty percent chance you want to take?' Asked Lola. 'Yes,' replied Mark. 'So how come you ran so fast when you found out you had the trait?' Asked Lola. Mark was silent, then he said, 'it doesn't matter now.' 'Yes, it doesn't matter now but, you need to apologise to Alhaji, you had no business talking to him like that. I am sorry to say, your wife's family are also ignorant,' said Lola. Mark changed the subject and asked Lola when she was due, it worked out that Lola is due four weeks after Mark's wife in July. 'It was nice talking to you Lola, we will speak soon,' said Lola. 'Thanks for calling Mark and yes, we will speak soon.' Lola hung up the phone and hoped that she never hears from Mark again.

Lola felt disgusted when she realised that she had done nothing all morning. Ada had texted to tell her lunch break was at one so, she had to leave now to get to Selfridges on time. Stefan also called to confirm he will be back at three. Lola decided after lunch with Ada, she will go straight home. Monday morning in the office was a waste of time, she was sure it wouldn't get any better. The pregnancy was making her so tired. Lunch with Ada was awkward, Ada just wanted to talk about Mark and his wife. Lola had to pretend to be interested in Mark's marriage, after a while, Lola had to ask Ada to change the subject. Ada apologised for being insensitive. 'You don't have to apologise, Ada, Mark disrespected a close friend of mine so, I rather not talk about him,' said Lola. Lola told Ada about the conversation she had with Mark this morning. Ada didn't like Mark but, she put up with him because of her friend. They spent the rest of the lunch hour talking about sickle cell awareness. After lunch with Ada, Lola popped into Holland & Barrett's, she had run out of vitabiotic pregnacare Plus. Lola believed this might be the reason she had been feeling so tired. She headed home, she hoped that she could get more work done if she worked from home. Lola arrived home a little after two in the afternoon, she sat at the computer to read and reply all her email, she must have fallen asleep, she woke up when Stefan came through the door. 'Hello, sleepyhead, I can see you are working very hard,' said Stefan. 'I am just resting my eyes,' replied Lola. 'How was your meeting?' Asked Lola. 'It went well, the CEO tried to play hardball, but, he back down towards the end of the meeting, he is coming down to the fashion house on Friday, if he likes the setup we have here, he will sign a five-year contract with us, I ordered Chinese, I hope you are hungry?' Asked Stefan. 'I am starving; I didn't eat much for lunch.' replied Stefan. They both sat on the couch in front of the telly and ate the Chinese food. 'It will be an early night for me,' said Stefan. 'I still have emails to reply to,' said Lola. 'You can do that tomorrow,' replied Stefan.

The next day Lola needed to get all her work done, she left her mobile phone at home. If her office phone rings, it could only be about work or an emergency. Lola had replied to all her emails, there was an email for an acceptance quote, the deadline was yesterday. She called the company, even though it was just a small contract, Lola always dealt with all her potential contracts in the same manner. Lola called the company, apologised for missing the deadline and she even undercut the quote she had already given as a gesture of goodwill. The company excepted Lola's quote, and they both agreed to a meeting the next day to sign the contract papers. Stefan will have a fit when he finds out she is completing the order at cost price. Lola went down to the factory to speak to the line manager. Lola needed this new order expedited, she would not make any money on this order so, it made sense to spend less time as possible completing the order. The line manager was being argumentative, he claimed his workers could not stop to complete her order first. Lola was furious with his lack of respect for her authority, she told the line manager he will be looking for a new job if the order is not ready by the end of the week. The line manager was so angry and told her, he would speak to Stefan. Lola told him to speak to whoever he likes but, she wants the order finished. Lola was furious, how dare he question her authority. The line manager stormed passed Lola, almost brushing against her, as she was walking back to her office, she noticed Stacey and the line manager talking in the reception area. Lola walked past them both and headed back to her office, she was about to make a phone call when there was a knock on the door. Come in, shouted Lola. The line manager came into her office. I want to apologise for my behaviour earlier, I am having a bad day, I had no right taking it out on you. Lola told him, no apology was necessary, she wants the order completed by the end of the week. The line manager assured Lola the order will be ready, and he left the office. Lola was wondering if the conversation the line manager had with Stacey had anything to do with his sudden change of mind. Stacey must be up to something; she would never take her side unless there was something in it for her. Lola called Stefan to find out what he was doing for lunch. Stacey would have updated him about the argument between her and the line manager. Lola was sure that Stefan would mention it at lunch. 'We will have to have lunch in my office, I can’t leave the office, I am waiting for an urgent fax from China. I will order a takeaway, what do you fancy?' Asked Stefan. 'Surprise me,' replied Lola. 'Okay, I will see you in one hour,' replied Stefan.

Stefan ordered pasta from Bocca di Lupo, their pasta bolognese is so delicious. 'Stacey said you shouted at the line manager?' Asked Stefan. 'I never shouted at him, I told him, if my order is not ready by the end of the week, he would be out of a job,' replied Lola. 'Is this the same order you are completing for next to nothing?' Asked Stefan. 'Yes, that is why I don't want too much time wasted on it,' replied Lola. 'That's fair enough,' said Stefan. 'How's your pasta?' Asked Stefan. 'It's delicious,' replied Lola. 'What else did that busybody Stacey have to say?' Asked Lola. 'She said nothing else,' replied Stefan. 'That's hard to believe,' said Lola. 'Are you calling me a liar?' Asked Stefan. 'No, I know that Stacey would not leave it at that,' replied Lola. 'Well, she didn't have a choice because I told her to mind her own business, Lola, you have a low opinion of me, don't you?' Asked Stefan. 'Do you think I would take sides with my employees over my wife to be, without hearing from you first?' Asked Stefan. 'I am sorry Stefan but, Stacey has been trying to pull my strings for months and I have been doing my best to ignore her,' replied Lola. 'Stacey is my former wife's friend so; she will be resentful towards you, if she doesn't allow it to affect her work, I will put up with her attitude until she crosses the line. As for the line manager, he is an agency worker and if his work is not satisfactory, get rid,' said Stefan. 'I don't know what Stacey said to him, but, he came to apologise after and promised the order will be ready before the end of the week,' said Lola. 'Are you happy with his response?' Asked Stefan. 'Yes, I am,' replied Lola. 'Good, case closed, just call me Judge Judy, the male version,' said Stefan. 'Judge Judy is brilliant; no comparison,' replied Lola. 'If I wasn't in the rag trade, I would have made. a fantastic Judge,' said Stefan. 'Yeah, right replied Lola, last week you would have been a fantastic chef, this week it's a fantastic Judge, next week you will tell me, you would have been a fantastic brain surgeon,' replied Lola. They both laughed. Stacey called to say the fax had arrived from China. 'I need to read over the contract with a fine-tooth comb, I will be home late tonight; I will be conference calling with the CEO in China. What will you be doing for the rest of the day apart from upsetting my staff?' Asked Stefan. 'Stefan, stop being facetious,' replied Lola. 'I won't be upsetting anyone else today because I am going home,' Lola said with a big smile on her face. 'Thank God for that,' replied Stefan. 'See you later part-timer, the way you are carrying on, anyone would think you are sleeping with the boss,' said

Stefan. 'Well I am, it's what I call friends with benefits, love you, Stefan,' she said as she hurried out of the door before he could say anything else. Stefan always wants to have the last word Lola arrived home, and she checked her phone, she had four missed calls, two from her mother, Alhaja called from Nigeria and there was a UK mobile number she didn't recognise. Lola called the number back, she is eager to find out who's number it belongs to, a woman answered the phone. 'Hello,' said the woman. 'Hello,' replied Lola. 'I received a missed call from this number,' said Lola. 'Oh yes, I called you,' said the woman. I am Mark's wife Ella, I called to thank you for coming to my wedding reception, I got your number from Ada, I hope you don't mind? Asked Ella. 'Not at all,' replied Lola. 'How's married life treating you?' Asked Lola. 'It's good,' she replied. I hope we can become friends?' Asked Ella. 'Any friend of Ada is a friend of mine, said Lola. 'Ada and I went to high school together in Lagos,' said Ella. Lola was feeling so uncomfortable with this phone call, she didn't want to be friends with Mark's wife, but, she didn't want to appear rude either. 'Will you please come to my baby shower? Ada is organising a baby shower for me next month, she doesn't know I already know,' said Ella. Lola couldn't think of a good enough excuse to decline the invitation. 'I will send you the details by text,' Ella didn't even wait for a reply from Lola. 'Please don't tell Ada I invited you, I don't want to ruin her surprise,' said Ella. 'Well, I will speak to you soon, thanks for returning my call, have a good afternoon,' said Ella. 'You too,' replied Lola. 'Bye,' Ella put the phone down, Lola still had the phone to her ear, she was so angry with herself that she didn't have the nerve to decline the invite to the baby shower. Lola also returned Alhaja and her mother's phone calls, Lola's mother is not happy that, she is going to Ella's baby shower, Lola told her mother not to worry, that she will find a reason not to go, she was angry with Ada for giving out her number without asking her, she had not spoken to Ada for two weeks. Ada sent Lola text messages, but, there has been no invite for lunch. Lola was missing her lunch dates with Ada, it was a good reason to leave the office, having lunch with Stefan happens only on rare occasions.

Ada has taken sickle cell awareness to the next level, she is doing a skydive to raise awareness. Ada is doing the skydive on world sickle cell day which falls on the nineteenth of June, she emailed Lola the sponsorship form, Ada was a little disappointed that Lola refused to talk about her experience with sickle cell anaemia for her Facebook Page. Lola had said no because she was not ready to talk about that part of her life, it was still too painful. Ada tried to hide her disappointment, she felt Lola wasn't committed to creating sickle cell awareness as she claimed to be. Lola put Ada's sponsorship form up in the office canteen, hoping that people will sponsor Ada. A few people asked Lola what sickle cell anaemia was, Lola explained what it was and the effects of the blood disorder. People were very interested and wanted to know if the blood disorder was contagious. After a week of putting the sponsorship form up, Lola had already raised one hundred and fifty pounds. Stefan promised to double the amount she raised from the fashion house. Lola took the form to Stefan and told him she had raised one hundred fifty pounds so far. 'That's great, I will double the amount,' said Stefan. 'Oh no, I am donating one thousand pounds,' replied Lola. Stefan jaw dropped, 'one thousand one hundred and fifty pounds then,' said Stefan. 'Thank you, Stefan, you are so generous,' said Lola. Lola scanned the sponsorship form back to Ada. Lola also sent Ada a message to confirm how she would like the sponsorship money sent to her. Ada responded and thanked Lola for her continuous support. She also sent Lola a link to her JustGiving page.

Lola was meeting with a potential client and the receptionist called to tell Lola that, she has a visitor waiting in reception. Lola asked the receptionist who the visitor was, the visitor's name is Ada replied the receptionist. Lola was surprised to learn that Ada was in reception, apart from text messages and emails, Lola had not seen Ada in two weeks, she was wondering why Ada came to see her unannounced. Lola told the receptionist that, she was in a meeting and will be unavailable for one hour. Ada said she would wait. After the meeting, Lola went to the reception to see Ada. Ada was on Facebook updating her page. Ada stood up and hugged Lola, Lola hugged her back. 'I am so sorry, I kept you waiting,' said Lola. 'No worries,' replied Ada. Lola took Ada to her office. 'It's been awhile, look how big you are getting.' said Ada. Lola smiled, 'to what do I owe this pleasant surprise visit?' Asked Lola. 'I am so sorry I have not been in touch, I have been so busy setting up my new business,' said Ada. 'New business,' said Lola in a surprised tone. 'Yes, I no longer work at Selfridges, I am opening my makeup business in Camden,' said Ada. 'That's fantastic news, why didn't you tell me you were planning to start your own business?' Asked Lola. It wasn't planned, I was talking to Ella, Mark's wife, she was so impressed with the makeup I did for her and her friends at her wedding, Ella said I could make a lot of money running a makeup store,' said Ada. 'With all Ella's friends and associates, she knows all the top names in Nollywood and she has friends in the ITV studio, I have spent the last four weeks completing makeup courses,' said Ada. 'My new store opens next week, and I would like you to be my guest of honour,' said Ada. 'I would love to, I am so proud of you,' said Lola. 'Thank you,' replied Ada. Lola and Ada spent the rest of the afternoon talking about Lola's new business idea. Ada is a fantastic makeup artist, Lola knows she will be a success, Ada is also planning to go to Nigeria to make a name for herself, even though Ada was so busy with her new business, she remained committed to creating sickle cell awareness. Ada will incorporate sickle cell awareness with her new business, Ada's business idea was very impressive; she had thought of everything. The only thing that Lola was worried about was that the business seemed to rely on Ella's contacts.

Lola tried to explain to Ada that, she had to be more in control of her business contacts, but, Lola didn't seem to understand what Lola was getting at and she was on the defensive. 'All I am saying is that you can't depend on Ella's contacts to run your business,' said Lola. Ada changed the subject and invited Lola to Ella's surprise baby shower. Lola had to pretend that she didn't already know about the baby shower. Ada told Lola that, Mark won't be at the baby shower, so she didn't need to worry about seeing him. 'I am not worried about seeing Mark, Mark and I are history,' replied Lola. Lola tried to hide her annoyance from Ada, as much as she liked Ada, Ada could be very insensitive sometimes and she often spoke without thinking. Lola and Ada talked about the opening, Lola volunteered to pay for all the food and drinks for the opening. It was a little after four o'clock when they both finished organising Ada's opening day. Lola couldn't believe how late it was. 'What time do you want me to come to the shop next week?' Asked Lola. 'Can you make it for ten in the morning?' Asked Ada. 'Yes, I will be there at ten,' replied Lola. Lola's opening was a great success, people were in and out of the shop all day. Ada had her first contract with a local theatre company, Ella was carrying on as if she was the business owner. Lola helped Ada with the adverting of her new business, she didn't want Ada thinking her business would not be a success without Ella.

Chapter Twelve

Lola was getting ready to attend Ella's baby shower, Lola was having second thoughts about going, she kept making up excuses to get out of going. Stefan had to convince Lola to attend because she had no clue it was her baby shower too. Ada had sworn Stefan to secrecy, he had also helped Ada to invite people that Lola knows, his sister-in-law will also be at the baby shower. Lola called Ada, 'what time are you going to get to my house?' Asked Lola. 'Lola, I have to run a few errands, I will meet you there,' replied Ada. 'What? You invited me to the baby shower and now you want me to go on my own,' shouted Lola. 'Lola, you will be fine; most of the people coming to the baby shower were at the opening of my makeup shop,' said Ada. 'Okay,' said Lola, and she disconnected the call. 'I am sick and tired of Ada,' shouted Lola. 'What has she done now?' Asked Stefan. 'She has blown me out, now she wants me to turn up to the baby shower on my own, I am not going, I can't believe Ella and Ada talked me into going in the first place; I am sick and tired of them both,' she said. 'You don't mean that Lola?' Asked Stefan. 'I do,' she replied. 'Stop acting like a spoilt child,' replied Stefan. 'I don't know why you all are trying to make me do something I don't want to do.' said Lola. 'No one is forcing you to do anything, Ella has done nothing to you for you not to like her and Ada, they both have been nothing but good friends. If going to the baby shower is making you unhappy, I will go on my own,' said Stefan. 'Why are you going?' Asked Lola. 'Someone has to make an excuse for your absence,' replied Stefan. 'You don't have to make an excuse, I can just call Ada and tell her I am not going, but if you are going, I will go too, I won't feel awkward with you there,' said Lola. 'That's my girl,' said Stefan. Stefan and Lola arrived at the baby shower, Lola had the shock of her life when she found out that the baby shower was for her too. Stefan had invited people from the Fashion House, his brother and his wife were also there, it was a fabulous Evening; even Ella didn't know about the double baby shower.

Lola was busy getting the rooms ready for her mother and Temi. Temi had been looking forward to moving to London, he couldn't wait for the end of the school term, his last day at school was so emotional for him and his friends,

knowing he might not see them again. His teachers had a big send-off party for him at school, Temi's best friend Kenny was also going to London for the summer holidays. Lola had invited Kenny and his mother to her wedding. Stella, Kenny's mother is an old friend of Lola's when she lived in Lagos. It was Lola's intention to ask Stella to be her maid of honour, but she ended up asking Ada instead. Just as Stefan had pointed out to Lola, Ada has been a good friend to her. Ada was so excited about being Lola's maid of honour and this will be her first time going to Italy.
Temi and Lola's mother arrived that Evening, Lola went with the driver to pick them up from the Airport, she has been looking forward to seeing her son, she couldn't believe how much he had grown in less than six months. She gave him a big hug, Temi had been looking forward to seeing his mother again. 'Mummy, I missed you,' he said, 'I missed you more,' Lola replied. Lola then greeted and hugged her mother, she seemed to have aged a lot since the last time she saw her. Lola's mother has been suffering from high blood pressure, the death of her husband had taken its toll on her. The only thing keeping Lola's mother going was the responsibility of looking after Temi. Lola hoped that the doctors

in London could get her mother's high blood pressure under control with the right medication. Temi was telling his mother about the send-off party he had in school. Lola didn’t get the chance to speak to her mother, she will have to wait till Temi goes to bed, he loves to be the centre of attention. Stefan had arrived home when they got back, he had ordered Chinese for everybody. After dinner, Stefan and Temi went to play a computer game. Lola and her mother spent the rest of the Evening talking and planning the upcoming wedding, there wasn’t much to plan because Stefan had made all the arrangements. Lola and her mother still needed to go shopping, Temi needed a suit to wear on the big day. Temi was restless after playing all them computer games with Stefan. Lola took him to his room, he had his own bathroom; he had a quick soak in the bath and put on his pyjamas. Lola read him a bedtime story, he was asleep before she got halfway through the story; she put the book away and turned his light out and went to join her mother in her room. Lola’s mother had just finished having a shower and was sitting on her bed reading her bible. Lola sat on the bed next to her mother and told her about the baby shower, her mother already knew about it. The baby shower was in the gossip magazine in

Lagos. Lola was not happy about that, she is a private person, sharing her baby shower with Ella wasn't a good idea after all. Ella is a socialite so, everything she does or says will be in the local papers in Lagos. Lola was still talking to her mother when she realised that, her mother was sleeping. Lola smiled and got up, she turned off the light and closed the door behind her.

It was a small wedding, just close family and friends since it was both their second marriages, they didn't want a big fuss. Although, Stefan had pulled out all the stops; they were getting married in Verona. Verona is a city in Northern Italy, Veneto region, with a medieval old town built between the meandering Adige River. It's famous for being the set of Shakespeare's "Romeo and Juliet." Lola looked beautiful in her wedding dress, she had made it herself. Ada did her makeup, Stefan barely recognised her when she came into the Villa hall. The venue was so romantic; Stefan had booked Villa Zambonina for the weekend. All the fifty guests invited were staying at the Villa too. Stefan twin sons were his best men; Ada was Lola's maid of honour. It was a beautiful ceremony, everything went to plan. Lola felt like a queen and she couldn't wait to say, 'I do' to Stefan. Stefan had promised to take Lola to the Maldives for their honeymoon. Lola insisted they go after the birth of her baby. Lola was so looking forward to going to the Maldives, the Maldives looked so exotic on television.

Stefan was getting ready for work, he checked his work phone, he had over twenty messages on it. Lola did not allow him to take the phone with him to Italy, she wanted no one to interrupt her wedding. Lola instructed Stacey to make all the decision in Stefan's absence and under no circumstances must she call him for anything. Stacey couldn't believe they were both getting married, she never thought Stefan would marry Lola. Stacey had told the receptionist that Lola is just a trophy girlfriend like Bisi was and that was the rumour Stacey was spreading around the Fashion House. There used to be an agency staff called Gino, he liked Lola and remained loyal to her. Gino told Lola what Stacey had said, she promised him she would not act on any of the information he gave her, but she made Stacey uncomfortable whenever the opportunity arose.

Lola spent the day with her mother and Temi baby shopping, they went to the Mamas and Papas store in Watford. Lola's mother fell in love with a vintage style pushchair, it was beautiful but, Lola thought it was a waste of money as she couldn't imagine herself using the pushchair. she ended up buying a three in one pushchair, you can use it as a carrycot, a car seat and a pushchair. The pushchair would fit in the boot of any car and its lightweight. It was more practical than the vintage style pushchair. Temi was getting bored with shopping and he was also hungry, he wanted to go to McDonald's, he loved the Big Mac's. After eating at McDonald's, Lola decided it was time to go home, her feet were swelling up, and she didn't want to walk around any more shops. They all got in a taxi and headed home, as soon as Lola got home, she went to lie down, her feet were killing her, and she needed to elevate her feet to reduce the swelling. Lola was just about to drop off to sleep when her phone rang. Ada's name popped up on the phone display, Lola ignored the call. When the phone stopped ringing, Ada left a message asking Lola to call her back, she also said Ella had just given birth to a baby girl.

Lola slept for about two-and-a-half hours', she was feeling much better, her feet were no longer hurting. She reached for her phone and called Ada. Lola was at the hospital with Ella, Lola asked Ada to pass the phone to Ella so, she could congratulate her. Later that Evening Ada called round to see Lola. Ada told Lola that Mark and Ella's baby is so beautiful and healthy. Mark was disappointed because he wanted a boy. Lola said she wanted to see Ella in the hospital because she didn't want to go to her house. Ada stayed for dinner and they talked about her plans to go to Nigeria. Ada had a makeup workshop sponsored by a top Nollywood star, she was so looking forward to the event.

Stefan dropped Lola off at the hospital, Lola wanted Stefan to go with her to see Ella but, he was going to a meeting. 'I don't know why you can't go later or even tomorrow?' Asked Stefan. 'I need to go now,' replied Lola. 'Why?' Asked Stefan. 'They might discharge Ella and the baby later or tomorrow,' replied Lola. 'You can see her at home,' replied Stefan. Lola was now getting frustrated with Stefan. 'I don't want to go to her house, let's leave it there,' replied Lola. 'All right, Lola, I will see you later, give my regards to Ella,' replied Stefan. 'Will do,' replied Lola.

Ella's baby girl was so beautiful. Lola was trying to work out who the baby looked like. Mark is a handsome man and Ella is beautiful too. Lola stayed for just over half an hour, Ella had so many visitors coming in and out. I guess that is the price for being well-known. The nurse came into Ella's private room to remind Ella that she can only have three people in the room at one time and she also complained about the noise. It doesn't matter where Nigerians congregate when they, get excitable outsiders will think they are fighting because they get louder and louder. This was Lola's key to leave after all everyone else was reluctant to leave. Lola opened the door, Mark was standing in the doorway she, congratulated him on the birth of his newborn baby and brushed passed him. Mark asked her why she was being evasive? 'I am not being evasive,' replied Lola. 'What made you feel I am?' Asked Lola. 'It would seem as if you are desperately trying to avoid me,' replied Mark. 'You, are being paranoid,' replied Lola. 'Why can't you move on?' Asked Mark. 'I have moved on and I am happily married to Stefan,' replied Lola. 'If that's the case, why are you always sniffing around my family?' Asked Mark. 'I couldn't care less about you and your family,' Lola screamed at him. 'Tell me why you are here?' replied Mark. 'I was just being a friend,' replied Lola. 'That's you all over, isn't it? Do you think you are better than everyone else? You might as well not have come at all, but that's not good enough for Lola because it would have shown your dishonesty,' said Mark. 'What are you talking about?' shouted Lola. 'Why are you here?' Mark shouted at her. Lola was so angry; she was finding it difficult to fight back the tears. 'I came to see Ella and the baby that's why I am here,' replied Lola. 'Ella is not your friend, so why come?' Asked Mark. Lola couldn't answer that question, she didn't really want to come, Lola felt obligated after sharing a baby shower with Ella, so many things were running through her mind. This was all Ada's fault; Ada will have to choose who she wants to be friends with. Ada is the only link between her and Mark, Lola wants the link broken. Lola just realised that Mark was still standing in front of her waiting for an answer to his question. Lola said in a calm voice, she was very sorry her coming to see Ella and the baby have upset him and she will stay out of their lives in future. Mark called her a hypocrite, 'it's not your visit to Ella that upset me, it's your dishonesty, you are always making out you are better than everyone else,' said Mark. 'Mark, where did all this animosity come from? You have the nerve to talk about dishonesty, did you tell Ella that you have the sickle cell trait?' Asked Lola. 'Ella could have had the trait too, and then there would have been a fifty percent chance that your baby had sickle cell anaemia,' said Lola. 'Lola, you are a big fool, what has that got to do with you? What I discuss with my partner is none of your business, did you discuss having the sickle cell trait with your husband?' Asked Mark. 'Tell me, when is the best time to have that conversation with your girlfriend, at the start of the relationship or just before marriage? Ella's pregnancy wasn't planned, so talking about our genotype was not a priority. When did you have the sickle cell talk with Stefan? Has Stefan taken the test?' Asked Mark. 'Mark, for your information, Stefan and I talked about sickle cell anaemia at the start of our relationship because it's a very important part of my life and Stefan didn't need to take the test because sickle cell anaemia only affects people from African descendant. I have nothing more to say to you, have a nice life,' said Lola. 'You too,' replied Mark. Lola stormed off down the corridor, her heart was beating so fast, she was furious. 'Why did I let Mark get me so wound up?' she asked herself out loud. Lola's head was spinning, she felt like her air supply was being cut off, she needed fresh air. Lola was walking up and down the corridors, she was having difficulty finding the exit, the last thing she heard before she fainted was her phone ringing.

Lola woke up in a bed in A&E. 'What is going on?' Asked Lola. The nurse told her to stay calm, you fainted so you are under observation. 'What’s happened to my baby? Asked Lola. 'Nothing, the doctor has been waiting for you to come around, so they can check you and the baby are doing okay.' replied the nurse. 'How long have I been out cold? Asked Lola. 'Just under fifteen minutes, don’t worry your husband is on his way,' replied the nurse. 'How did he know I was here?' Asked Lola. 'He called you before you fainted, the porter answered the phone asked him to come to the hospital right away,' said the nurse. 'We will do a scan and check the baby’s heartbeat,' said the nurse. 'Why' Asked Lola. 'You took a heavy fall when you fainted, and it would seem you landed on your stomach So, the scan is just precautionary,' replied the nurse. 'I need to call my husband,' said Lola. 'Don’t worry, he is on his way,' replied the nurse. 'Why am I feeling contraction pains?' Asked Lola. 'Let’s go for the scan, after that we can carry out more tests, try to relax, everything will be okay,' said the nurse. Lola was so worried, she knew something was wrong, she felt as if the doctor had already done the test while she was out cold, but, they were waiting for her husband to turn up before they gave her the bad news. Lola was crying, she remembered the argument she had with Mark, she vowed never to speak to him again, he is the reason she is lying in A&E, she prayed for her baby's health, the contractions were becoming more frequent. The doctor came and told Lola that the nurse needs to take her for a scan. Lola said she wanted to wait for her husband, the doctor said he couldn't wait any longer, the nurse came into the room and asked Lola to sit in the wheelchair and she wheeled her to the ultrasound department. Lola was now crying; the nurse was also trying to console her. The nurse asked her to stay calm or she won't be able to do the scan. Lola took off her lower garments and lifted her blouse. The nurse put this cold substance on her stomach and was about to do the scan, then the nurse told Lola to put on her clothes that, she can't do the scan because the baby is coming. Lola screamed, the baby can't come now, It's four weeks early. The nurse rushed Lola down to the maternity ward and placed her in a room. People were just coming in and out, they were talking to her, but, she couldn't hear anyone. One nurse gave her gas for the pain, it didn't feel as if it was working. The nurse told Lola to push, on the second push, the baby was out. Lola heard her baby cry and then her baby was taken out of the room. Everyone left the room, and she was all alone. The nurse came into the room to ask if she wanted to have a shower. 'Where is my baby?' Asked Lola. 'Your baby boy is fine, he is in the neonatal ward, he was having difficulty breathing, but he is okay now,' said the nurse. The nurse took Lola to the bathroom so, she could have a shower, 'when you're done, I will take you up to the neonatal ward,' the nurse said. Lola felt all alone, so much has happened in such a little time, this is not how she thought she would have her baby. Lola felt so alone why is Stefan taking so long to get to the hospital? Lola was crying, 'why did I let Mark get me so wound up?' She asked herself out loud. The stress must have been too much for my baby. Lola was deep in thought; she didn't even notice when Stefan walked into the room. Stefan called her name, Lola ran over to him and she sobbed. 'Where were you when I needed you the most?' Asked Lola. 'I am so sorry Lola, I came as fast as I could, I got held up in traffic,' replied Stefan. 'Where is our baby?' Asked Stefan. Lola was still crying; she didn’t answer him. Stefan thought the worst had happened. 'Where is our baby,' Lola? Asked Stefan again. The nurse then told him to calm down, your baby is in the neonatal ward, he had difficulty breathing, but he is okay now. I have been trying to get your wife to have a shower, so I can take her up there. Stefan then pulled Lola away from him, 'I am so sorry I couldn’t get here any sooner, I have been going out of my mind with worry. Everything will be okay now,' said Stefan. Lola stopped crying, 'it’s all my fault,' she said. 'It’s not your fault,' said the nurse. 'Mothers have premature babies all the time, no one knows why it happens, you can’t feel guilty for your baby coming early, you can do all the right things during pregnancy and things can still go wrong. I have worked as a nurse in this maternity ward for ten years and I have seen so many mothers have premature babies, all blaming themselves. Your baby is perfect and a very handsome boy,' said the nurse. 'A boy,' said Stefan. All this time he had not even realised the sex of the baby; he was hoping for a girl. Stefan asked Lola to have her shower so, they can see their son. Lola stopped crying and went to have a shower. The nurse took them both up to the neonatal ward. Lola could not pick up her baby, he was in an incubator and he had wires with electrodes stuck to parts of his little body. The electrodes detect every activity of his heart, breathing and temperature. The nurse told them not to worry about all the wires, your son is doing just fine. Lola took his little hand and her baby grabbed onto her finger as if his little life depended on it. Lola and Stefan sat in the neonatal ward next to their baby's incubator for hours. The doctor came in and reassured Lola that, her baby will be fine. Even though the baby is four weeks early, he is doing well, and the baby is on oxygen just for precaution. The doctor said he was planning to take the baby of the oxygen machine tomorrow and he is confident that their baby will breathe on his own. Lola was feeling numb; she couldn't believe she had just given birth. The nurse asked her to follow her back to the ward, she will need to express her milk with a breast pump. Her baby is not strong enough to be breastfed right now. Lola didn't want to leave the neonatal ward, she kept thinking

something else would go wrong. Lola was crying again, she kept blaming herself. It was all too much for her, if only I didn't have that argument with Mark, this wouldn't have happened. I didn't want to visit Ella; I should have followed my instincts. Stefan told her to stop blaming herself and this was not the time for if only. Lola was too distraught to argue, but, she knew Stefan was right. The nurse escorted them to the ward and showed her how to use the pump to express her milk. Stefan sat with her while she was trying so hard to express her milk. Lola filled up all the bottles given to her, Stefan labelled them and put them in the fridge so that the milk is available when her baby needs it. Stefan was feeling rejected by Lola, even though Lola had not said it, he felt as if she was blaming him for not being at their baby's birth. Lola has been showing hostility towards Stefan since he got to the hospital. Stefan told her he was going home to check up on Temi and Lola's mother. All they knew was that Lola had given birth. 'There is no need for you to come back tonight, you might as well stay home and bring Temi and my mother to the hospital tomorrow if that is not too much trouble?' Asked Lola. 'How dare you speak to me in that tone,' said Stefan. Lola was the only person who could get under his skin. 'I know I wasn't there for you today but, that's no reason to be horrible and for your information, it's no trouble at all,' said Stefan. Stefan left the room, he knew Lola was hurting and looking for someone to blame, the kindest thing to do, is to rise above it. Stefan just couldn’t understand why Lola was shutting him out. Lola cried, she needed Stefan more than ever, she didn’t mean to push him away. The nurse came in and tried to console her. 'Where is your husband?' The nurse asked. Lola could barely speak and just continued to sob.' 'I have sent him home,' Lola replied.' Why?' Asked the nurse. 'I don’t know,' said Lola. 'Do you want me to call your husband?' Asked the nurse. 'No, I will speak to him tomorrow,' replied Lola. 'You need to sort whatever is the matter with your husband, you both need each other right now and your baby needs you both,' said the nurse. Lola was still sobbing. 'You need to pull yourself together, your baby is doing well, he is getting stronger and stronger,' said the nurse. Lola felt guilty, for thinking of herself instead of her baby. 'I am going up to see my son, he is my priority,' said Lola.

Lola sat with her son holding his little hand and praying for him to get better. The nurse told Lola to go back to the maternity ward and force herself to sleep, she is of no use to her baby if she is tired. The nurse told her that, her little boy is in safe hands and they would let her know if there are any changes. Lola went back to the

maternity ward and curled up on her bed, she was missing Stefan. Lola picked up her mobile and called Stefan, he answered the phone. 'How are you, Lola?' Asked Stefan. 'I am okay, just tired,' she replied. 'I am so sorry Stefan, I didn't mean to be horrible to you,' said Lola. 'I know you didn't, I am so sorry I wasn't there for you when you needed me,' said Stefan. 'It's not your fault Stefan, I had no right pushing you away. I am so sorry, said Lola. 'That's okay Lola, do you want me to come back to the hospital?' Asked Stefan. 'No Stefan, it's late Temi and my mother needs you at home,' replied Lola. 'How's Luca?' Asked Stefan. 'Who is Luca?' Asked Lola. 'Our little boy,' replied Stefan. 'I can't believe you have already given our baby a name without discussing it with me,' said Lola. 'Don't you like the name, Luca? I think he looks like a Luca,' said Stefan. 'What does Luca mean?' Asked Lola. 'It means the bringer of light,' he replied.
She paused for a few seconds, her silence worried Stefan. 'Hello, are you still there?' Asked Stefan. 'Yes, I am. I am just getting used to the name Luca,' said Lola. 'Do you like the name,' Asked Stefan. 'Yes, I love the name,' replied Lola. Lola and Stefan talked for a while longer, Lola fell asleep with the phone still over her ear.

Lola woke up the next morning feeling ready to take on the world, she had a quick shower and went to use the breast pump after she filled and labelled her bottles she went up to see Luca. Lola had fallen in love with the name Luca, the nurse told Lola that the doctor is happy to take Luca of the oxygen, the doctor will be on the ward in two hours. Lola called Stefan and told him to get to the hospital as soon as possible, Luca is coming off the oxygen in two hours she was excitable. It delighted Stefan to hear her refer to their baby as Luca. We are on our way; we will be there in half an hour. Lola went back to sit with Luca, she was so looking forward to holding her baby for the first time.

Lola's mother and Temi were so excited about meeting Luca for the first time. They both took turns holding his little hand in the incubator. Temi wanted to know why he was so small, Lola told him he was too eager to meet him, so he came a little earlier than expected. Lola told him not to worry because Luca eats a lot and he will soon grow bigger and stronger. The doctor came in and took Luca's temperature before taking him out of the incubator, he explained to Lola and Stefan that their baby needs to regulate his own body temperature and breathe on his own without oxygen. The nurse took Luca out of the incubator and passed him to Lola, she showed her how to hold her baby the Kangaroo-style. Kangaroo-style is skin-to-skin care, the technique allows an adult to hold the infant, and the infant learns to sniff out its mother's milk. Luca was still hooked up to the breathing apparatus to check his vital signs. Luca is doing well; both his breathing and temperature are stable. The doctor is happy for Luca to sleep in a crib, but his vital signs still need to be monitored.

Lola was in the maternity ward packing her things away for Stefan to take home, she was looking forward to sleeping in her own bed tonight. Luca was putting on weight and he was getting stronger, the doctor said Luca would have to spend at least two weeks in the hospital before he could go home. Stefan went home to bring Lola's mother and Temi to the hospital. Lola and Stefan were in and out of the hospital for two weeks. Lola went up to the neonatal ward to give Luca his feed. While she was feeding Luca, the nurse came in to take a blood sample from Luca heel, it's called the heel prick. A blood sample is taken and used to check for any serious health issues, the blood sample is taken on the fifth day of a baby's birth. The nurse explained to Lola that the test results will come back within six weeks and that they will only contact her if they need to do a re-test or if their baby has a serious health issue. Stefan came in to tell Lola that her mother and Temi are in the waiting area, they were both eager for a cuddle with Luca.

Luca is now two weeks old, and he had put on a lot of weight and getting stronger. The doctor said he could go home, he could now suckle, and Lola has been breastfeeding him. Lola was so excited that she could take her baby home. Stefan had finished Luca's room for his homecoming. Luca was such a good baby, all he does is eat, sleep, dirty his nappy and he only cries when he is hungry. Luca went to sleep after his feed, Lola also fell asleep, she had not had a good night's sleep since the birth of her baby. Lola asked her mother to watch the baby while she went to sleep. Stefan was in the master bedroom on the phone talking to his mother, Lola walked in and Stefan asked if she wanted to go to sleep? 'Luca is sleeping now so, I thought I should use this opportunity to get some sleep as well.' replied Lola. 'That's a good idea, I am off to the study, my mother sends her regards,' said

Stefan. 'Send her my love,' replied Lola. Stefan kissed her on the lips and told her he loved her. 'Love you too,' replied Lola. Stefan left the room and closed the door behind him. Lola slept for a little under three hours, she must have been so tired, she only wanted to sleep for forty-five minutes to an hour. She got up, the heaviness of her breast reminded her she needed to feed her baby. She went to Luca's room; her mother was in there feeding him. 'What time did Luca wake up?' Asked Lola. 'He woke up about ten minutes ago,' replied her mother. 'Has he got enough milk in that bottle?' Asked Lola. 'Yes, he has, you will need to express more milk and put it in the fridge, I have used the last bottle,' said Lola's mother. Lola went off to express her breast milk, by the time, she had finished filling up the bottles and returned to Luca's room, he was fast asleep again. Temi came into the room, he was excitable so, Lola led him out of the room, he had been playing computer games with Stefan, according to Temi, he had beaten Stefan. Stefan joined Lola and Temi in the living room. Temi was telling his mother how he beat Stefan, Lola's phone rang, it was Ada. 'Lola, how are you?' Asked Ada. 'I am okay, thank you,' replied Lola. 'I arrived this morning, how's Luca? Is he home yet?' Asked Ada. 'Luca is fine, and he is home now,' replied Lola. 'Oh great, I will come and see you all this Evening, I have something to tell you, I don't want to tell you over the phone,' Ada said. 'Oh, really, I will look forward to seeing you later,' said Lola. 'What I will tell you will be worth waiting for,' replied Ada. Lola put the phone down, she hasn't got the energy for visitors, but, she was keen to find out what Ada had to say. Lola knew it had something to do with Ella and Mark. Ada must have been reading the gossip magazines in Lagos. Lola went to check on Luca, he was in his cot, sucking his figure. 'Are you hungry again little man? It's a good job I don't have to buy my breast milk, or I would be bankrupt by now,' she said and laughed to herself. She picked

Luca up and took him to the living room and breastfed him, Lola's mother and Stefan were cooking in the kitchen. Stefan was trying to teach her how to cook an Italian meal, but, Lola's mother wanted to cook it her way. Lola decided not to get involved with their cooking arguments. It was great having two good cooks in the house, but, deciding who would cook on the day could turn into a domestic argument Stefan has been working from home since the birth of Luca, his way of helping was to cook but, the constant arguing with Lola's mother over who would cook was becoming tiresome.

The doorbell rang, it was Ada. Lola went to open the door, no one else seemed to have heard the doorbell. Lola was so glad to see Ada. 'Ore, I have missed you,' said Ada. 'I have missed you too,' replied Lola. 'Oh my God, look how big Luca has got. Have you been overfeeding him?' Asked Ada. 'Luca eats like a horse, its non-stop with him,' replied Lola. 'You both look well anyway,' said Ada. 'Thanks' replied Lola. Ada sat down and cradle Luca in her arms. 'He is so handsome, just like his father, where is everyone?' Asked Ada. 'They are all in the kitchen, let's go into the kitchen, it's too quiet in there. I hope they haven't killed themselves,' said Lola. Lola and Ada both laughed at Lola's joke. Ada knew about the kitchen dominance, they walked into the kitchen, Stefan was showing Temi and Lola's mother something out of an Italian cookbook. 'Good Evening Ma', said Ada, 'Good Evening my daughter, how are you?' Asked Lola's mother. 'I am fine Ma,' replied Ada. 'How was your trip to Lagos? I can't believe you are back so soon,' said Lola's mother. 'My business trip to Lagos went well thank you,' replied Ada. 'That's great,' replied

Lola's mother. 'Hi Stefan,' said Ada. 'Hello, Ada, I am so glad you are back, Lola has been missing you, I don't know why she speaks to you every day,' said Stefan. 'You know what Lola is like, she is needy,' replied Ada. 'Hello,' I am standing here you know,' shouted Lola. 'Yes, we can see that,' replied Stefan. 'I haven't got time for you now, I need to talk to my friend,' said Lola. 'See what I mean, you have been talking on the phone every day for two weeks, but you both still find things to talk about,' said Stefan. 'Stefan, your jealousy will get you nowhere, why don't you call a friend?' She rolled her eyes at him and walked off, Stefan laughed and took Luca from Lola, 'you can talk to your friend now, I don't want my son listening to gossip,' said Stefan. They both laughed and left the kitchen. 'I will call you guys when dinner is ready,' Stefan shouted out.

Lola and Ada were sitting in the living room talking, 'guess what?' Asked Ada. 'What? Asked Lola. 'You won't believe this,' replied Ada. 'Mark's baby has sickle cell anaemia,' said Ada. 'What?' Shouted Lola. She was in shock, I thought you said Ella had the AA blood type?' Asked Lola. 'She lied to Mark,' replied Ada. 'Mark never told Ella that he had the sickle cell trait, he insisted that Ella took the test because he didn’t want a child with sickle cell anaemia. Mark even told Ella that his ex-girlfriend had the sickle cell trait, and that was the reason he dumped her, I guess he was referring to you,' said Ada. 'Mark is so absurd and calculating, with all his lies, what has he achieved? He now has a wife that lied to him about her genotype and now they both have a child with sickle cell anaemia,' said Lola. 'If only they were honest with each other, they could have talked about their options. How come this has only come out now?' Asked Lola. The baby's blood test results came back a few weeks ago, showing that their baby has sickle cell anaemia,' replied Ada. 'Oh my God,' said Lola. I feel so sorry for Mark and Ella; I can imagine what they are going through right now. I think I need to see them both if only to reassure them,' said Lola. 'I don’t think they will appreciate a visit from you,' said Ada. 'Why?' Asked Lola. 'Ella is still in shock, and Mark is not speaking to her, I have tried several times to call Ella but, she won’t answer or return my calls,' said Ada. 'I believe she is preparing to go to Nigeria with the baby, according to the gossip magazine, her parents want her to bring the baby to Nigeria, they are so convinced that, they can cure the child in Nigeria,' said Ada. 'The child would be better off over here,' said Ada. 'That's a matter of opinion,' replied Lola. 'Anyway, Ella needs the support of her family, Mark is an arsehole and very unreliable. I am going to Ella's house tomorrow, she needs a friendly face but, I am not even sure if she will see me. I will let you know how I get on tomorrow,' said Ada. 'Please do,' replied Lola. Stefan came in to tell them the food is ready, Lola and Ada headed to the kitchen. Lola had lost her appetite. 'Don't you like my cooking?' Asked Stefan. 'I love your cooking, I am not hungry, I will eat it later,' replied Lola.

Ada was telling Lola about the live debate she had on Facebook while she was in Lagos, the debate was about sickle cell anaemia and malaria. Ada had to clear up a well-known myth that, people with sickle cell don't get malaria. Lola interrupted her, 'I was also under the impression that people with sickle cell anaemia don't get malaria?' Asked Lola. 'That is not true, the malaria parasite cannot live in a sickled red blood cell for long because the body senses that sickled red blood cells are improperly formed, so the body destroys as many sickled red cells as possible. If a malaria parasite is in the sickled red cell, it will also destroy it before it can cause any malaria symptoms so, a person who has sickle cell anaemia, the malaria symptoms are minor or no symptoms at all,' replied Ada. 'Wow, you learn something new every day, said Lola. 'You sure do, it's getting late now, I will phone you tomorrow and let you know if I get to see Ella,' said Ada. 'I will expect your call. Good night Ada,' 'Goodnight Lola.'

'What is the matter?' Asked Stefan. 'Nothing,' replied Lola. 'You have been acting strange all Evening,' said Stefan. 'Mark and Ella's baby has sickle cell anaemia,' said Lola. 'Oh really? How did that happen? I thought you said, Ella did the test, and she does not have the trait?' Asked Stefan. 'That is what she told Mark but, she lied, Mark didn't tell her, he has the trait so, they both lied to each other,' replied Lola. 'That was stupid of them both,' said, Stefan. 'I know, I can't believe how ignorant, they both were,' replied Lola. 'There is not much they can do about it now, they will just have to live with the consequences of having a child with sickle cell anaemia,' said Stefan. 'With all the research nowadays, the symptoms of sickle cell anaemia are manageable with medication but, Mark is not talking to Ella right now; Ella needs his support,' said Lola. Lola couldn't hold back her tears, 'I can imagine what Ella is going through, finding out your baby has sickle cell can be so devastating,' said Lola. Stefan held Lola in his arms and ask her not to cry. 'I know you don’t like Mark and neither do I but, we must put our feelings aside and do all we can to support them,' said Lola. 'If you say so Lola, you know I will do anything for you,' said Stefan. 'I love you, Stefan,' 'I love you too, Lola.' 'I can hear Luca crying,' said Stefan. Don’t worry, my mother will attend to him, make love to me Mr Coite,' said Lola. 'With pleasure, Mrs Coite,’ he carried Lola to the master bed and made love to her.

Ada called Lola early in the morning to tell her that, Ella and her baby had travelled to Lagos. Ada saw Mark at their house, he had been drinking and the house was a mess, he was so horrible to Ada, and he told her to leave and never come back. Stefan tried to call Mark but, he refused to answer his phone. Lola was on the internet looking for cures for sickle cell anaemia. Ada had told her about the bone marrow transplant. Lola wants to help Ella, Lola didn’t understand why Ella lied about her genotype, but, she knows about the stigma surrounding people with sickle cell anaemia or the trait. The bone marrow transplant is the only known cure for sickle cell anaemia. Lola had mixed emotions she didn’t know there was a cure for sickle cell, she was thinking about Babatunde, if only I knew, I could have saved my baby. Lola called Ada, 'I have been reading up about the bone marrow treatment, how come adults and children die of complications of sickle cell? Asked Lola. 'The bone marrow transplant has serious risks attached to it and it's only offered if a person has had a stroke, acute chest syndrome and frequent sickle cell crisis,' replied Ada. 'That makes no sense,' replied Lola. 'The pharmaceutical companies seem to make millions treating the symptoms, instead of investing in an affordable cure. We are in the twenty-first century, we can send people to the moon but, we can’t find a widely affordable cure for sickle cell anaemia,' replied Lola. 'Lola, it’s not that simple, even with the bone marrow treatment, we don’t have enough black and Asian people willing to donate blood let alone bone marrow. Unless you have a perfect match within the family, it would be very difficult to get a perfect match among a non-family member and even with a perfect match, the recipient body can still reject the bone marrow, said Ada. 'Why don’t more black and Asian people donate blood or bone marrow? Asked Lola. 'It’s a good question but, it’s a complex question to answer. I believe it’s down to people’s traditions and culture,' replied Ada. 'That is so stupid, it's very important that people should give blood and register to donate bone marrow, this selfless act will save lives, not only for people with sickle cell anaemia, it would help anyone with a life-threatening disease,' said Lola. 'We need to get hold of Ella and tell her what we have discovered, I am sure the bone marrow transplant will cure her baby,' said Lola. Ada told Lola that, she is going to Lagos in three weeks’ time, I will go to Ella's mother's house, I am sure she will tell me where to find Ella,' said Ada. 'I hope so,' replied Lola. Lola could hear Luca crying, 'I must go now, it's time for Luca’s feed, I will call you tomorrow or come round if you are not busy,' said Lola.

The following morning Lola got a letter in the post asking her and her husband to book an appointment, so they could discuss the results of the first screening blood test. When Lola read the letter, she could just about breath, the letter didn’t state what life-threatening disease Luca has. Lola went to the hospital, she was not willing to wait to book an appointment, she wanted to know now what was wrong with her baby. Lola ran to her mother’s room and asked her to look after Temi because she needs to find out what is wrong with Luca. Wait for us, said Lola’s mother. No, I am going on my own, replied Lola. 'What about Stefan, have you called him?' Asked Lola’s mother. 'I will call him on my way to the hospital,' replied Lola. Lola was getting irritated by her mother’s questioning, she was not in the mood for answering questions. Lola grabbed Luca’s baby bag and ran out of the house. She was standing outside when she realised she had not called a taxi. Lola went back in the house and called a taxi and went to fetch the pushchair, her mother was hovering around her not knowing what to do or say. 'We are coming with you to the hospital, I won’t let you go on your own,' said Lola's mother. Lola wasn't in the mood to argue, she looked at Luca, who was asleep in her arms. 'What have I done to offend God?' Lola asked her mother. 'I don't know my daughter, maybe it's nothing serious. 'The nurse said six weeks ago that they would only contact me if my baby has a life-threatening disease,' said Lola. 'Have faith, my daughter.' Lola was about to respond, but, she heard the taxi sounding his horn outside, 'let’s go, the taxi is here,' said Lola.

They arrived at the hospital, Lola went to the reception area to ask for direction to the department on the letter. The lady at the reception desk asked if she has an appointment. Lola told her that, she doesn't need an appointment, the lady told her she needs to book an appointment. Lola became hysterical at that point. 'What I need is to see a doctor right now,' replied Lola. She told the lady at the reception that, she would not leave the hospital until she has seen the doctor. The receptionist called security to come and remove Lola because she was causing a scene. Lola couldn’t care less; she was sobbing her heart out. Temi was trying to console her, Luca was also crying, and Lola's mother was trying to console them both. The security officer turned up and walked over to Lola and asked her what the problem was. Lola told him that her baby has a life-threatening disease, and no one wants to help her. The security officer didn't understand Lola response, he went over to the receptionist, the receptionist was waving Lola letter at him. The receptionist looked furious, the security officer took the letter from the receptionist and walked back over to Lola and told her to follow him. Lola refused to move. The security officer then told her that his wife works in the Oncology department where her letter came from, the security officer said he will call his wife to come down and see her. Lola's mother was full of gratitude for him showing compassion towards them, the security officer led them to a quiet area of the hospital while he called his wife, the security officer's wife was the lady that took Luca's heel blood sample. Lola is happy to see her, she hugged the security officer and thanked him as she walked off with his wife. Lola asked the nurse what was wrong with her son, 'I will take you to see the doctor, he will explain everything to you,' replied the nurse. 'Is my son going to die?' Asked Lola. 'No, your son will not die,' replied the nurse. The nurse-led them all to a room and asked them to wait while she gets the doctor. Lola's mother asked Lola if she had called Stefan. Lola looked shocked, with all what has been going on, she had forgotten to call him. She searched her handbag for her phone, there were seven missed calls from Stefan. She dialled his number and told him they were all at the Chelsea and Westminster Hospital. Stefan was in a meeting, but, he excused himself and told Stacey to take over the meeting.

The doctor came in and gave Lola the shock of her life, your son has sickle cell anaemia. 'How can he have sickle cell anaemia? I have the trait, but Luca's father is white,' said Lola. The doctor told Lola that, sickle cell anaemia mainly affects people of African, Caribbean, Middle Eastern, Asian and Mediterranean origin and from her last name, he can conclude that her husband has an Italian heritage so, your husband must have the trait and that is why your son has sickle cell anaemia,' said the doctor. Lola was just staring into thin air; she was finding it difficult to take in what the doctor was telling her. Lola couldn't believe history was about to repeat itself, the thought of losing Luca to sickle cell anaemia is unbearable. Stefan walked into the office, Lola was crying hysterically, our son has sickle cell anaemia,' she screamed. 'How did that happen? Sickle cell anaemia is not contagious, is it?' Asked Stefan. Stefan looked at the doctor for an answer, the doctor then told Stefan that he has the sickle cell trait. 'I don't think so somehow,' replied Stefan. The doctor asked Stefan if he had taken the test for sickle cell anaemia. 'No, I didn't think there would be a reason for me to have the test, as far as I am aware no one in my family has sickle cell anaemia,' replied Stefan. The doctor told Stefan that his family members can be carriers without their knowledge. Unless they take the test, they can pass the trait onto their children. 'I have two sons and they don't have sickle cell anaemia,' said Stefan. 'If the mother of your sons does not have sickle cell, your sons can still be carriers so, I suggest you get your sons and yourself tested,' said the doctor. 'What will happen to my son? Is he going to die?' Asked Lola. 'No, we are more medically advanced now to deal with the symptoms of sickle cell anaemia. Your son will be on folic acid to help make new blood cells and antibiotics to prevent infections. If your baby is in pain, you can use pain relief or massage the affected areas. Your baby won't be able to tell you where the pain is so, a full massage might help. If your child's pain is more severe, bring him straight to the hospital. Children with sickle cell anaemia are fast-tracked through A&E. If you have any problems, come straight to this ward. If you have any more questions, please call me or one of my colleagues,' said the doctor. 'What about the bone marrow treatment?' Asked Lola. The bone marrow treatment is mainly used for children that have severe cases of sickle cell complications, children that might have had a stroke, acute heart problems or severe pain,' replied the doctor. 'I will not wait for my child to develop all these complications, I have already had a child that died of sickle cell anaemia,' replied Lola. 'How old was your son when he died?' Asked the doctor. 'Babatunde was three years old, he had a stroke,' replied Lola as the tears were pouring down her face. Stefan held her hand, and he assured her that nothing will happen to Luca. 'Luca will have the bone marrow treatment, we will not wait for any complications to develop. I will spend my last penny if I have too,' said Stefan. The doctor told Lola and Stefan that, apart from the risk involved in the treatment, getting a perfect bone marrow match is the hardest thing to achieve, with their ethnic background. The doctor gave them all the advice they needed to care for Luca and he also said if they needed any more information about the bone marrow treatment, he would do all he can to help them. Lola and Stefan thanked the doctor for seeing them today and for all the reassurances he gave them. The nurse was outside attending to another patient, Lola walked over to her and thanked her for all her help. She told Stefan how the nurse had come to her rescue in the reception area. My name is Natalie, anytime you need my help, please call me. Natalie gave Lola her number, Lola missed called Natalie’s phone number, and she asked Natalie to save her number, Lola had a strange feeling she will need her help again. Natalie reminded her, she has an appointment booked with the midwife in two weeks and that she must keep all the appointments. Natalie stroked Luca's cheek and said don't worry little man, the Lord is your strength. As they walked past the reception area, Lola glanced over to the reception desk and the lady was sitting there staring at them. Lola rolled her eyes at her and continued walking. Lola's mother caught the look Lola gave the woman and told her to ignore her, one day she will be in a position where she needs someone to show her compassion, then she will know how it feels to have people turn their backs on her. Stefan looked confused, he didn't understand what Lola's mother was talking about, Lola put her hand in his and said I will tell you later.

Stefan was on the phone with his mother, he wanted to know if anyone in the family had sickle cell anaemia, his mother didn't know what sickle cell anaemia was. He explained to his mother that, he is a carrier and so either her or his father had the trait. Stefan knew he had to speak to all his brothers and sisters, not only did he have to tell them that his son has sickle cell anaemia, he also needed to find out which one of them or their children would be a perfect match to be a bone marrow donor. Stefan called Gianni, to tell him about Luca. Gianni is devastated, 'how can this be happening to you guys?' He said. 'I don't know,' replied Stefan. 'How is Lola?' Asked Gianni. 'Not so good, Lola has already lost a child to sickle cell anaemia, and she thinks it will happen again,' replied Stefan. Gianni has a soft spot for Lola, the simple fact she made his little brother happy, was enough for him, this could be a setback for them both, if Lola gets depressed, Stefan would slip back into that dark place again. 'Stefan, is there anything I can do?' Asked Gianni. 'Yes, I need a bone marrow match for Luca, that is the only cure for sickle cell anaemia,' replied Stefan. 'What is a bone marrow test? Asked Gianni. 'It's a simple blood test that determines your tissue type', replied Stefan. 'Don't worry Stefan, the whole Goite family will do the test,' said Gianni. 'Thanks, Gianni, I must go now, I need to check on Lola,' said Stefan. 'Send my regards to Lola, tell her we are all thinking of her,' said Gianni. 'Will do,' replied Stefan.

Chapter Thirteen

Creating sickle cell awareness has become a big part of Lola's life, it brought Lola and Ada even closer together. Lola had to get up very early she was going with Ada to Norwich. Today is the day Ada will do her skydive, she kept on postponing the event every time she felt nervous. Ada couldn't put it off any longer because the time frame given to complete the jump was about to expire. Lola was also feeling nervous, it would be the first time she has left Luca since she found out he had sickle cell anaemia, her mother told her to go with Ada because she needs a break. Lola didn't want to let Luca out of her sight, she thought something might happen to him. Dupe had told her she would never know happiness, ever since then it has been one heartache after the other. Lola's mother told Lola that, it's not Dupe's doing, she doesn't have the power to curse anyone. Lola's mother believes destiny played an important part and blissful ignorance. 'If you knew what you know now, would you have changed anything about your life with Stefan? You are so much in love with Stefan, would you have left him if you knew he had the sickle cell trait?' Asked Lola's mother.

Lola thought long and hard, 'I don’t think I would of; I love Stefan, I wouldn’t have been able to turn my feelings off just like that. Having a child with sickle cell anaemia is not the end of the world, children with sickle cell anaemia are also a gift from God, they just need extra special care,' replied Lola. Lola picked up her son and kissed him on the forehead so far, Luca has been on the healthy side of sickle cell anaemia, he has had pain crisis but, nothing serious, his hands and feet swelled up once and Lola’s mother gave him a massage to help the blood flow, the pain relief the doctor gave also helped to relive the pain. Lola did her best to prevent Luca from catching any infections, anyone in the family that was feeling unwell had to stay away from Luca. If Luca caught an infection, it could bring on a crisis. Lola’s mother has the doctor’s phone number just in case Luca got sick. Stefan was working from home so, Lola felt comfortable leaving her baby with her mother and Stefan. 'My phone will be on all the time so, please call me if you need me,' said Lola. She went to the Study to tell Stefan she was off to Norwich. Stefan told her not to worry, Luca will be fine. 'Hurry back Lola, I don't know if I can wait any longer, I am missing you already,' said Stefan. Lola could feel his hardness, I am missing you too,' replied Lola, she smiled at him and said, 'I will be back before you know it,' said Lola. 'I hope so, we can practise making more babies,' said Stefan. Lola couldn't believe what he had just said. 'Would you want to have more babies knowing we both have the sickle cell trait?' Asked Lola. 'Why not? You haven't given me a little girl yet,' replied Stefan. 'Don't you think it's irresponsible?' Asked Lola. 'No, I don't, it's a fifty percent chance we could have a baby without sickle cell or even the trait and that is a chance I am willing to take,' replied Stefan. 'We will talk about this when I get home, I can't even believe you are even contemplating such a silly idea in your head,' said Lola. 'Lola, why is it a silly idea? I am offended that you think having another child is a silly idea, do you regret having Luca? Asked Stefan. 'No, I am just thinking about the emotional and financial implications,' said Lola. 'Well, don't worry, we are in this together,' said, Stefan. 'Let's not fight over this Stefan, we need to talk about this when I get back,' said Lola. 'Love you,' said Lola. 'Love you more,' replied Stefan.

Ada knocked on the door and Lola went out to meet her, 'come on Lola we are running late,' said Ada. 'You are running late; I have been ready and waiting for you,' replied Lola. 'Okay, I am running late, let's get going,' said Ada. Lola was still thinking about what Stefan had just said although, she liked the idea of having a baby girl to make their family complete, she didn't think she had the strength to have another baby with sickle cell anaemia. Worrying about Luca all the time has taken its toll. If not for her mother, she would not have been able to cope. Ada noticed that Lola was in a world of her own and asked her what was the matter? 'Are you worrying about Luca?' Asked Ada. At that point, Lola realised that she had not thought of Luca for a good thirty minutes. 'Yes and no,' replied Lola. 'What does that mean?' Asked Ada. 'I am thinking about something Stefan said,' replied Lola. 'What did he say? Asked Ada. 'Stefan wants to have another baby,' replied Lola. 'What is wrong with that?' Asked Ada. 'What if the baby has sickle cell anaemia?' Asked Lola. 'Lola, it's a big what if? You're not having a baby right now but, it's something to think about, you need to talk this over with Stefan, there's a cure for sickle cell anaemia and you and Stefan can afford to pay for it so, I don't see a problem here. Let's concentrate on me surviving today's jump out of a plane. I am still thinking about that stupid Nigerian man who said I was helping to reduce the population of Nigeria, by jumping out of the plane and killing myself all in the name of sickle cell awareness,' said Ada, 'Ada, you must rise above stupid comments like that from stupid people. People can be so callous, just because they are not brave enough to do something, they belittle your efforts just to make themselves feel better about themselves,' said Lola. 'Lola, I know you're right, it's just that he had so many people on Facebook liking his comment,' replied Ada. 'Just ignore all the ignorant comments and concentrate on all the good feedback and comments from the people that appreciate your efforts. Your passion for sickle cell awareness is admirable, I am so proud of you and so are thousands of others. There is so much ignorance surrounding sickle cell anaemia and we need to create more awareness, my blissful ignorance got me into this predicament I am in today,' said Lola. 'Ada, you will jump out of this plane today and you won't kill yourself, not on my watch anyway,' said Lola. Lola and Ada burst out laughing, Lola told Ada that when she completes the jump and upload the footage to Facebook, everyone will be so proud of her and that ignorant Nigerian who made that stupid comment will be put to shame. 'I read on the internet that, Nigeria has the highest number of children born with sickle cell anaemia so, they should be your biggest supporters.' said Lola.

They took almost two-and-a-half hours to get to Norwich; it was a Sunday, so the traffic was not too bad. The closer Ada got to Norwich, the more nervous she got. Lola kept glancing at her phone, just to make sure she had not missed a call. Lola had the urge to WhatsApp Stefan but, she didn't want to come across as overbearing so; she decided against it. She promised her mother she would not call her because her mother got upset and accused Lola of not trusting her to look after Luca. Lola called Temi instead, he was playing on the computer with Stefan. Mother, 'I can't talk to you, I have just beaten Stefan at this game,' said Temi. Lola heard Stefan say in the background that, he was just letting Temi win. Stefan was so useless at the computer games and Temi loved playing with him because he knew he could beat him. 'Okay, I will speak to you guys later,' said Lola.

Ada had to change into overalls and she had to wear a helmet, after getting changed the video man came to interview her, Ada was finding it very difficult to speak due to her nervousness. Lola watched Ada board the plane, Ada turned around and waved to Lola. At that moment, Lola was so proud to call Ada her friend.

After thirty minutes, Ada landed with the parachute, it was a proud moment for her. Lola ran to her and hugged her and asked how was it? 'It was so scary but; it was a wonderful experience, an experience I won’t be repeating,' said Ada. Ada has a certificate to prove that she did the skydive. On the way back to London, Ada gave Lola a blow-by-blow account of her skydive, Ada was so proud of herself and so was Lola. Ada dropped Lola off at home. Lola felt relieved to be home, she had been so worried about Luca. Lola went to her mother’s room; Luca was cooing on her bed. 'How is Luca? Asked Lola. 'Luca is doing okay; he has just woken up,' replied Lola’s mother. 'Luca is hungry; do you want to feed him?' Asked Lola's mother. 'No, I need a shower,' replied Lola. 'Okay, my daughter, come back and tell me how Ada got on with the skydive,' said Lola's mother. 'Okay, mother,' said Lola as she closed the door behind her. Stefan and Temi were in the living room watching a Disney movie, to be honest, Temi was watching the movie, Stefan was fast asleep. Stefan claimed to be resting his eyes. 'I am going for a shower, then we need to talk,' said Lola. Stefan headed towards the kitchen to cook dinner. 'Lola, have you eaten already? Asked Stefan. 'No,' replied Lola. Everyone sat at the dining table for dinner. Stefan had cooked pasta, it tasted delicious as usual. Lola told them all about Ada's skydive. Lola was so proud, 'I don't think I could have jumped out of that plane, I would off wet myself on the way down, I don't know what Ada will do next in aid of sickle cell awareness,' said Lola. 'Well, whatever Ada does, I guess you will be right beside her egging her on.' replied Stefan. 'That's for sure,' replied Lola. For someone that does not have sickle cell anaemia, she will do almost anything to create awareness of the disorder. 'On the way back from Norwich Ada, was talking about swimming with sharks,' said Lola. 'That I would like to see,' replied Stefan.

Ada couldn't wait to get home, she wanted to upload her skydive video and pictures to her Facebook page. Ada called to tell Lola that, she has had a lot of good feedback from her skydive and people just keep liking my post. 'That's fantastic,' said Lola, 'I am logging in now, oh, my God, I have liked the post and I am reading all the comments; the skydive made an impact. I like the comments from those that wanted to know what sickle cell was. I am so proud of you; the skydive was a brilliant idea; it has driven a lot of traffic to your sickle cell awareness page,' said Lola. 'Thank you, Lola, how are you?' Asked Ada. I am okay,' replied Lola. Did you have that talk with Stefan?' Asked Ada. 'No, not yet, but, we will later tonight,' replied Lola. 'Make sure you do,' replied Ada. 'I am writing a post tomorrow on my page about bone marrow donors. I need to encourage more Africans, Asians and mixed-race people to donate blood and register themselves on the bone marrow register,' said Ada. Due to the lack of donors from people from ethnic backgrounds is making it difficult to cure life-threatening diseases. 'Often people refer to sickle cell anaemia as a disease why is that? Asked Lola. 'It's down to ignorance, sickle cell anaemia is a blood disorder, you don't hear no one referring to cancer as a disease. It's so annoying, ignorance itself is a disease that needs eradicating,' said Ada. Ada told Lola that she went to a sickle cell group at Kings College Hospital, she sat and listened to a member of the group explain how he's always made to feel like a drug addict when he goes to the hospital for stronger pain relief, just because the pain they feel is not obvious to the medical professionals, they imply they are faking it for stronger drugs.

Lola and Stefan lay in bed talking about having another baby, Lola felt uncomfortable talking about having another baby. Stefan said regardless of Luca having sickle cell anaemia, he does not regret him being here and he knows, Luca will get a bone marrow transplant that will cure him of sickle cell anaemia. Lola couldn't argue with his logic, the only argument she could present was the emotional side of things, no parent wants to see their child in pain and bringing a child into this world that might have sickle cell anaemia is irresponsible. 'Lola, I am getting bored, let's talk about this another day,' said Stefan. 'Stefan, we must talk about this now,' replied Lola. 'Lola, I would rather talk about it another day, let's practice making babies instead,' said Stefan. 'Stefan, can you be serious for one minute,' replied Lola. 'I am being serious,' replied Stefan. Stefan turned over and caressed her, Lola always found it difficult to resist him. They made love and Stefan fell asleep. Lola lay on her side; she couldn't get the thought of having another baby with sickle cell anaemia out of her head. After so much tossing and turning, she fell asleep.

Chapter Fourteen

It's three in the morning and the sound of the phone ringing woke Stefan. Stefan's sister was calling from Atlanta; he took the phone call in his study because he didn't want to wake Lola up. Lola had tossed and turned all night, he knew she was worried and now that; she had got to sleep; he didn't want to disturb her. Stefan's sister was so excitable; he was having difficulty understanding what she was trying to tell him. It took a few minutes for him to work out that his sister was trying to tell him that her daughter has the same tissue type as Luca so, she would be a perfect match for him. Stefan was in shock; he couldn't believe what she had just told him. Gabriella married an African American so, her three children are mixed-race. The possibility of Stefan's sister's children being a perfect match for Luca was higher than any other family members because Luca is also mixed-race. Stefan ran into the bedroom with the phone shouting for Lola to wake up. 'What on earth is the matter?' Asked Lola. 'Tara has the same tissue type has Luca,' replied Stefan. Lola was looking confused. 'What are you talking about and who is Tara?' Asked Lola. 'Tara, my sister's daughter, the one who lives in Atlanta,' replied Stefan. Lola was now paying attention. 'Did you say Tara has the same tissue type as Luca?' Asked Lola. 'Yes, this is the best news ever,' replied Stefan. Gabriele was still on the phone, Lola snatched the phone out of his hand. Lola was asking Gabriele all these questions and not giving her the chance to answer the questions. Stefan told Lola to be quiet and give Gabriele the chance to speak. Stefan put the phone on loudspeaker. Gabriele told them that, Tara took the test last week and not only is she the same tissue type, she also has the rare Ro blood type. The Ro blood type is effective in treating chronic conditions like sickle cell anaemia. Lola was having difficulty taking it all in, she couldn't believe Stefan's sister's daughter would be the one to give Luca a new lease on life. Lola could not control her emotions and passed the phone back to Stefan, she was so overwhelmed and speechless. Tara was on the phone talking to her uncle, she was looking forward to coming to London to donate her bone marrow. They all agreed that she would come next year after she had graduated from high school. At least she would have the long summer holidays to recover before going to University. Tara was hoping to gain admission to the University of Oxford to study law. Stefan got off the phone with his sister and niece and went over to Lola, who was still sitting on the bed weeping and thanking God. 'I knew my family would not let me down,' said Stefan. 'I can’t believe this is happening, it the best news I have received in a long time, you and Gabriele are close but, letting Tara donate her bone marrow to Luca, it’s such a big deal,' said Lola. 'All my brothers and sisters offered their support too if any of their children had the same tissue type, they would be a donor in a heartbeat,' replied Stefan. Lola and Stefan could not go back to sleep so, they sat up and watched television. Lola’s mother knocked on the door, 'someone out here is starving,' she said sarcastically. 'I am coming mother,' said Lola. Lola got up to feed her baby, she also told her mother the good news. Both Lola and her mother were singing and praising God. Stefan poked his head around the living room door, 'I am off to work now, shall I book a table at Gianni’s restaurant?' Asked Stefan. 'Can’t we celebrate at home? Asked Lola. 'Yes, we can but, I need to tell Gianni the good news and I don’t want to do it over the phone,' replied Stefan. Okay Stefan, book a table,' said Lola. 'Is eight o’clock okay?' Asked Stefan. 'Make it seven, it's a weekday you know,' replied Lola. 'Seven it is then, see you all later,' said Stefan. Bye Stefan.' said Lola.

Lola called Ada to tell her about the good news, 'that's fantastic news, you are so lucky to have found a bone marrow donor. When will Luca have the bone marrow transplant?' Asked Ada. 'Not sure, we need to discuss our options with our doctor first, Tara will graduate from high school next year she wants to go to the University of Oxford so, it would be ideal for the procedure to take place here in London next summer,' replied Lola. 'Lola, I hope you will allow me to publish your story on my Facebook page? Your story will give hope to a lot of families and I hope it will encourage more people from African descendants to donate blood and bone marrow,' said Ada. Lola felt ashamed because, she had refused to allow Ada to write her story before but, Lola now realises that she is only in this predicament due to her own ignorance. Lola agreed for Ada to publish her story because she wants no one else to go through what she went through due to ignorance. When Lola first arrived in London, she had decided that she would not date a black man again just to rule out the fact she might have another child with sickle cell anaemia. Even though she had feelings for Mark, she used the possibility of them having a child with sickle cell anaemia to prevent them both from having a loving relationship together. Lola thought she had struck gold when she fell in love with Stefan, she didn't know people from the Mediterranean can inherit the sickle cell gene. It never crossed Stefan's mind to get tested for the sickle cell trait when Lola fell pregnant with his baby. After a lot of digging into Stefan's background, he found out that Stefan's father died from complications of sickle cell anaemia and Stefan was the only child to inherit the defective gene from his father. There is no excuse for ignorance about sickle cell anaemia, all the information about sickle cell anaemia is on the internet, all you have to do is Google the many sickle cell groups and ask for advice. There is only one way to avoid your children from inheriting sickle cell anaemia and that is getting to know yours and your partner's genotype. If you and your partner have the trait, it's important that you understand the financial and emotional implications of having a child with sickle cell anaemia. However, medical treatments for treating the symptoms of sickle cell anaemia is so advanced now, it's not all doom and gloom.

Tara graduated from high school with flying colours, she gained admission into her first choice, the University of Oxford. Tara donated her bone marrow to Luca, she is a very healthy girl, and she experienced none of the side effects of the procedure. It was the one thing Lola was grateful for; she didn't want Tara to suffer from any side effects for doing such a wonderful thing for her baby. Tara told her uncle she would donate again if she had to, it was a painless procedure, done under anaesthesia. Luca was in the hospital for three months, he needed lots of medical and nursing support while the stem cells engraft. About a month after the bone marrow procedure, the doctor noticed the first signs of engraftment, the red blood cell counts had risen. This showed that the transplant was making new blood cells. Luca could go home; he still needs regular follow-up appointments. Six months after the bone marrow procedure, the test showed that Luca no longer had sickle cell anaemia.

Lola supported Ada with the campaign to make bone marrow transplants available to adults and children that need it. It can be a very expensive procedure if you go private. The Nhs only consider the bone marrow transplant in children with sickle cell anaemia who have severe symptoms that haven't responded to other treatments. The risk of the bone marrow transplant for adults seems to outweigh the long-term benefits of the transplant. More research is necessary to reduce the life-threatening risk to adults and children so that, the bone marrow transplant can become an affordable cure for all sickle cell suffers. Pharmaceutical companies are just getting richer treating the symptoms of sickle cell anaemia. For every cure to a person with sickle cell anaemia, is a big loss to the pharmaceutical companies. People think it's a black person disease so finding a cure is less of a priority, what people fail to realise nowadays, is that there are lots of inter-racial-marriages and partnerships, the blood disorder is hereditary so, the blood disorder will no longer just affect black people. Sickle cell anaemia has been around for over one hundred years, it's unbelievable that we can now send people to the moon but, we can't find an affordable cure for sickle cell anaemia. Another big hurdle is getting people from ethnic backgrounds to donate blood and bone marrow for all life-threatening diseases. In the twenty-first century, ignorance is no longer bliss.

28480910R00174

Printed in Poland
by Amazon Fulfillment
Poland Sp. z o.o., Wrocław